## SPECIAL MESSAGE TO READERS

This book is published under the auspices of

**THE ULVERSCROFT FOUNDATION**

(registered charity No. 264873 UK)

Established in 1972 to provide funds for research, diagnosis and treatment of eye diseases. Examples of contributions made are: —

A Children's Assessment Unit at
Moorfield's Hospital, London.

•

Twin operating theatres at the
Western Ophthalmic Hospital, London.

•

A Chair of Ophthalmology at the
Royal Australian College of Ophthalmologists.

•

The Ulverscroft Children's Eye Unit at the
Great Ormond Street Hospital For Sick Children,
London.

You can help further the work of the Foundation by making a donation or leaving a legacy. Every contribution, no matter how small, is received with gratitude. Please write for details to:

**THE ULVERSCROFT FOUNDATION,**
**The Green, Bradgate Road, Anstey,**
**Leicester LE7 7FU, England.**
**Telephone: (0116) 236 4325**

**In Australia write to:**
**THE ULVERSCROFT FOUNDATION,**
**c/o The Royal Australian and New Zealand**
**College of Ophthalmologists,**
**94–98 Chalmers Street, Surry Hills,**
**N.S.W. 2010, Australia**

# ELUSIVE LOVE

Amelia has always been determined to marry for love . . . but with her elder brother dead and posthumously branded as a traitor, Amelia and her sister find themselves penniless and ostracised by society. When a relative contrives to put an '*eligible parti*' under an obligation to make Amelia an offer, Amelia has to decide whether or not to stand by her principles . . . and face the consequences of turning down what might be her only chance to escape her unbearable situation.

# KAREN ABBOTT

◆

# ELUSIVE
# LOVE

*Complete and Unabridged*

## LINFORD
*Leicester*

First published in Great Britain in 2008

First Linford Edition
published 2009

British Library CIP Data

Abbott, Karen.
  Elusive love.—Large print ed.—
  1. Love stories.
  2. Large type books.
  I. Title
  823.9′2–dc22

  ISBN 978–1–84782–640–4

Published by
F. A. Thorpe (Publishing)
Anstey, Leicestershire

Set by Words & Graphics Ltd.
Anstey, Leicestershire
Printed and bound in Great Britain by
T. J. International Ltd., Padstow, Cornwall

This book is printed on acid-free paper

# 1

'Darling Cookie, have you time to make up a small picnic for Clara and me?' Amelia Haverton coaxed as she burst into the kitchen of her home as if she were a nine-year-old instead of her stately twenty years.

Mrs Tranter threw up her hands in dismay. 'Eh, Miss Amelia! You mustn't go out dressed like that! What if someone should see you? Whatever would they think?'

Amelia glanced down at her oldest cotton gown. Undoubtedly, it had seen more wear and tear than it ought to have done, a fact borne out by its numerous patches and faint stains that not even Mrs Tranter's best efforts had been able to remove.

'I'm sure they would think it eminently sensible, Mrs Tranter!' Amelia responded, her lips puckering with amusement. She

1

smiled reassuringly at their faithful servant. 'It is such a lovely afternoon that I decided it would be just the thing to go down to the spinney to pick some blackberries ... and it is such a relief to be able to dispense with our mourning clothes at last ... and the fresh air will do Clara no end of good. I'm sure a bottle of your lovely lemonade and some of your delicious buttered scones will be as delightful as the Prince Regent's grand fête for our precious Duke of Wellington! But only if you have time, of course!'

'Of course, I have time! Anything that will bring a smile to Miss Clara's face, Miss Amelia. It's been a hard year for the pair of you.' And the future holds no better, she thought inwardly, her face clouding for the moment.

She pushed her dark thoughts aside and began to bustle about her kitchen. 'Now, how about some cold chicken, a few of these ripe tomatoes and some bread rolls?' she suggested, gathering together the items as she spoke. 'And how about Kate going with you? You never quite know who might be roaming the countryside since our poor soldiers have been coming home and finding no work for them to do. No? Then I'll set her to making some pastry for when you get back.

'Eh, it's all very well for the Prince Regent to spend a fortune on the so-called Peace Celebrations . . . and a fine time everyone had in London, I'm sure . . . but what does it mean to them who 'as been fighting for their country an' now feel as though they've been thrown on the scrap-heap? I'm sure the poor King would do something about it if he was in his right mind!'

'Sadly, you're quite right, Mrs Tranter. I thought exactly the same thing when I was reading it all out to you from *The Times*. Though I'm sure the Prince Regent will do his best to sort something out for them. Let's just be glad that that war is over and the war with America is soon to be at an end and no more soldiers will die in battle!' Amelia responded passionately.

'That, however, is the business of our politicians. Right now, my business is to give Clara something other than Cousin Blake's imminent arrival to dwell upon. She was as blue as megrim about it earlier today.'

'Ain't we all, Miss Amelia? Ain't we all?' Mrs Tranter agreed, shaking her head as she banged the stopper into the top of the bottle of lemonade. 'Eh, it was bad enough when Master Ralph was taken from us last year . . . but to have your dear papa follow him to the grave so soon afterwards was too much for any soul to bear! And now, this! What is to become of us, Miss Amelia?'

Mrs Tranter's voice ended in a wail as she quite uncharacteristically cast herself down on a kitchen chair and threw her apron over head, wailing loudly.

Amelia was thankful that their maid, Kate, was busy upstairs, preparing the bedrooms for her Cousin Blake, his wife, Louisa and their young son, Vernon . . . and their retinue of servants . . . who were coming to make an exploratory visit to Moreton Manor prior to becoming its next incumbents.

Not for the first time since the untimely deaths of their older brother and father, Amelia silently berated her and Clara's long-dead ancestors for their short-sighted policy in ensuring that the line of inheritance of the property would forever follow the male line. It hadn't mattered when Ralph was alive. He would have ensured that she and Clara had a home there until they were married and that they would be endowed with a sizeable dowry to enable them to make a satisfactory 'match'.

That, too, had been part of the shattering loss that she and Clara had had to come to terms with — along with the hasty withdrawal of a recent offer of matrimony from Amelia's suitor, the Honourable Frederick Hughes. 'Dishonourable,' Amelia couldn't help adding, each time she thought of him — which was hardly at all now that more than twelve months had passed. Now, with only the prospect of three thousand pounds each to be theirs either upon marriage or on attaining their majority at the age of twenty-one, they had small prospects of making a favourable match.

Not that she would ever marry purely for money, Amelia reminded herself, but she had imagined herself to be deeply in love with Freddie and had been devastated when he had withdrawn his suit.

'But my brother wasn't a traitor!' she had implored him. 'You know he couldn't have done anything like that!'

'Hmm, but you know the old saying, 'No smoke without fire',' Freddie had murmured uncomfortably, flicking an imaginary speck of dust off his sleeve as he avoided looking Amelia straight in the eye. 'I'm sorry, m'dear but it can't be done. Not the thing, you know, to taint your family line with dishonour!'

Now, just over a year later, Amelia

shook the unpleasant memory aside as she strove to encourage Mrs Tranter to resume her fortitude.

'I am sure we shall fare very well, Mrs Tranter!' she declared brightly. 'After all, Cousin Blake has allowed us to fulfil our year of mourning . . . and at Papa's funeral, he promised not to make us homeless.'

'Hmm! And a bag of moonshine that might turn out to be!' Mrs Tranter responded, her spirit reviving somewhat at the scent of battle. 'A right tartar that wife of his seemed to be! Mark my words, Miss Amelia! Things will change around here and no mistake about it!'

'Then we must make the most of the time we have left, Cookie, darling . . . and if we have to do some tip-toeing around for a while, then so be it!' Amelia said briskly. 'And, as I'm sure you and Kate need all your time to get everywhere ready for our guests . . . yes, 'guests', Mrs Tranter. Moreton Manor has always been a hospitable home . . . Clara and I will enjoy our little picnic to the full. Ah, here she is,' as her seventeen-year-old sister entered the kitchen. 'Come, Clara. You carry the smaller basket and I'll take this one.'

Feeling wonderfully liberated from the confines of their mourning clothes, the two girls happily set off through the kitchen garden, heading for the spinney. Casting aside the constraints that society imposed on young ladies of their class, they skirted the orchard and ran lightly across the lower meadow, their skirts brushing against the knee-high flowers that were gently waving in the bright sunshine, releasing their heady scents into the air.

Clara twirled around, her basket swinging from her out-stretched arm. 'Oh, Melie! I'd forgotten what it was like to feel so carefree! I swear I'll never wear black, purple or grey ever again! Oh!' She clapped her free hand to her mouth and looked up at Amelia with wide, repentant eyes. 'Is that being terribly selfish, Melie? It isn't that I've stopped caring about Ralph and Papa

. . . only one can't mourn for ever, can one?'

'No, indeed not!' Amelia assured her. 'Neither Papa nor Ralph would have had it so. We loved them dearly but I truly believe it is time to cast off our mourning clothes and our sorrow and look to the future.'

'Will society welcome us back, do you think?' Clara asked wistfully. 'I long to go to balls and soirées and have lots of beaux. Don't you?'

'It will be good to be free to do so when and whenever we wish,' Amelia agreed less enthusiastically, knowing that for Clara's sake, she must put aside her own misgivings. 'Maybe Cousin Louisa will sponsor us.'

Clara visibly brightened. 'Then their visit may not be as bad as we fear! Come on! I'll race you to the corner gate. Last there is a wet goose!'

With all pretence at decorum abandoned, the girls ran down the gently sloping meadow, their bonnets slipping off to the backs of their heads, revealing identical auburn curls escaping from the confines of the many clips that had held them in place and laughingly declared their race a dead heat. As Amelia opened the gate, Clara unceremoniously scrambled over the stile and leaped down into the country lane that led to the spinney.

Neither of them noticed the lone horseman who drew his cantering horse to a standstill up on the nearby upland. The Irish wolfhound that accompanied him had already prickled his ears as the sound of laughter and girlish chatter drifted in the late summer air.

The man's eyes sought the source of the unidentifiable words that still drifted towards him, and a flash of movement at the edge of the spinney caused his gaze to sharpen and an unaccustomed grin lightened his rather stern features. The movement had been a beribboned bonnet sent spinning to the ground by its owner's hand and now lay abandoned on the grass.

He saw one of them rummage in the hedgerow and pull out some sort of stick that she handed to her companion, a girl of slighter build than herself, and then repeat the procedure until another stick was found. She then bent down and lifted out the contents of two baskets, placing them out of his sight behind the trunk of a thick oak tree and handed one of the baskets to the younger one.

When they purposely approached the hedgerow in front of them and began to hook down its trailing tendrils with the sticks in their hands, reaching up with their free hand, his features relaxed even more. Of course! They were two village girls out on an afternoon spree picking blackberries, he realised, envying their carefree gaiety . . . or, to be more accurate, regretting that his own days of youthful exuberance had been cut short by the wars that had gripped their nation for as long as he could remember. The musical sound of their voices and laughter had ceased and, with some reluctance, he gathered his reins together.

'Come, Russ!' he bade his hound. As he pressed his knees into his mount's flanks to spur him into motion, he cast a last wistful glance over his shoulder and then galloped away, leaving the two girls industriously harvesting the shining black fruits in companionable silence, working their way along the hedge.

Amelia found herself humming a lively air, her spirit lighter than it had been for over a year . . . when a sudden yelp and scream from Clara shattered the peaceful scene.

Amelia whirled round in time to see Clara sprawling into the brambles a few yards away and two rough-looking men hovering over her.

'Hey! How dare you!' Amelia shouted, dropping her basket and hurrying towards her sister. One man had already grabbed Clara's basket from her and the other was scooping up the neatly wrapped picnic that Mrs Tranter had obligingly tied in a small checked cloth and one of the bottles of lemonade.

Enraged by the attack upon her sister, Amelia raised the stout stick that was still in her hand and began to flail it across the shoulders of the man nearest to her.

'Be off with you!' she cried, wielding her stick with a great degree of accuracy.

The man turned to face her and, for a moment, Amelia feared he was about to reciprocate the violence being directed towards him but, instead, he began to back away. His gaunt face bore a few days growth of unkempt stubble and his skin showed an unhealthy pallor that seemed at variance with its weather-beaten tan. He raised his arms to deflect her blows as he retreated backwards, half-stumbling over the rough ground.

His companion had paused at what he obviously considered to be a safe distance. 'Come on, Tom. Let 'em be!' he called out.

The man named Tom, clutching their

picnic to his chest, held an entreating hand towards Amelia as she continued to pursue him.

'I'm sorry, miss! Don't mean you no 'arm. Sorry, miss!'

His pace accelerated into an ungainly crablike shuffle, gaining speed as he felt the dirt track under his feet.

Conflicting emotions warred in Amelia's brain and she slowed her pace, but continued to brandish her weapon as the space between her and the two men widened. Only now did a frisson of fear begin to spiral within her and the sound of Clara's voice calling her name brought her to a standstill.

'Melie! Melie! Let them go! Come and help me get out!'

Amelia reluctantly dragged her eyes away from the retreating pair to look over her shoulder to where she could see Clara still sprawled amongst the brambles.

She looked back to where the two men were loping in an ungainly fashion down the dirt track and knew that they were intent only upon getting away. One had his hand on the other's shoulder, dragging his left leg. She frowned as she turned and ran back towards her sister . . . but her concern for their state dissolved away as her concern for Clara's welfare took over.

'Take hold of my hand, Clara, and I'll try to pull you out. Oh, you poor girl!' she sympathised as Clara struggled to get on to her feet. 'Thank goodness you fell backwards! Come, dear . . . Oh!'

Her words were cut off as a wolf-like dog darted past in seeming pursuit of the men, closely followed by a dark-clad horseman at full gallop.

The horseman paused momentarily, wheeling his mount in a tight arc as he called across, 'Are you all right? Did they harm you at all?' Keeping his mettlesome horse in control with his knees as he spoke, he freed one of his hands and gallantly raised his hat revealing short-cropped dark hair. Although he was more attentively attired than their two assailants, his clean-shaven face was as weather-worn as theirs and a vivid scar ran down his right cheek, marring his otherwise handsome looks. In spite of the fact that he was not wearing any sort of uniform, he had a distinct military bearing.

'N . . . no m . . . more than you can see,' Amelia stammered, her heart thudding by the surprise of his abrupt arrival and his rather sinister appearance.

The man's horse sidled and pawed the ground restlessly. Keeping him on a tight rein, the man gave a peremptory nod, his lips set in a firm line. 'Good! Hang on! I'll be right back!'

With no more ado, he gave his horse his head and was gone out of sight in a flurry of dust.

'Who was that?' Clara asked in amazement.

'I've no idea!' Amelia said faintly, her mind reeling. The swift events of the past few minutes seemed like the staccato, unrelated elements of a nightmare and she was unsure which had alarmed her the most. She pushed all three men out of her mind and turned her full attention back to Clara, hiding her inner turmoil with outwardly care and concern. 'Stand still whilst I disentangle these brambles from your dress . . . and your hair! You look as though you've been dragged through a hedge . . . which I suppose you have! Are you hurting anywhere, Clara?'

'I feel a bit shocked, I suppose . . . though it could have been a lot worse! They looked so fierce! Oh, Melie! I just want to go home!' Clara's demeanour crumpled as she wailed the last words and she fell into Amelia's arms, sobbing uncontrollably. She lifted her tear-streaked face to her sister, hiccupping, 'I was so frightened, Melie! I thought that the one you were intent on breaking his head was going to fight back and then come and finish me off! You were like an enraged vixen!'

'A buffle-headed one more like it!'

Amelia countered, with false cheerfulness as she picked up their remaining basket of half-spilled blackberries. 'I didn't stop to think of the possible consequences. And I'm sure they were interested only in stealing our food.'

She allowed her glance to drift towards the now deserted track that the two men and their would-be rescuer had taken, as she murmured philosophically, ' . . . and, from the look of them, they needed it more than we do!'

Unharmed though they were, Amelia had no more desire than her sister to linger in the vicinity and, with a subdued air, she briskly ushered Clara through the gate into the meadow and back home. At the top of the meadow, she cast an involuntary glance over her shoulder, wondering if their gallant rescuer would return as he had promised . . . but the area was as deserted as they had left it.

It was of no matter. If he did indeed return, he would rightly assume that they had safely returned to their home and, as his intervention had been too late to help them in any way, they did not owe him the courtesy of thanking him for his service. Turning away, she mentally shrugged, satisfied that no more was to be made of the matter.

The lone rider did indeed return. He thought at first that he had misremembered the place . . . but the patch of crushed blackberries reassured him on that score. He felt a sense of disappointment, followed by a stab of anxiety. Had they fled in distress? He absently figured the vivid red scar that ran from the outer edge of his right eye to the corner of his mouth. His mouth twisted ruefully.

It was enough to repel any of the gentler sex. A fact probably intensified by his impetuous pursuit of their attackers added to their distress? With a deprecating shrug, he acknowledged that the thrill of the chase had momentarily overcome his more chivalrous nature. The inevitable outcome of his years campaigning on foreign soil!

As his gaze rested on the trampled grasses and the disturbed hedgerow, the image of a tousle-haired young woman flickered in his mind and, gripping with an intensity that surprised him, he headed his horse in the direction of the village.

# 2

Four days later, the household was poised to welcome Blake Forrester and his family for a short visit. In spite of bitter thoughts about her imminent ousting from her position as 'lady-of-the-house', Amelia wanted her beloved home to be seen at its best and had zealously joined in the work of giving the manor house a thorough dusting and polishing, leaving no corner unswept nor any mat unturned.

'Can't we leave wet rags to moulder in unseen corners and hide a few dead rats under the floorboards to cause unwholesome smells?' Clara suggested with a glint of mischief in her eyes. 'I'm sure Cousin Louisa would turn up her nose in disgust and return to town at the earliest moment if she saw so much as a spider's web adorning the walls!'

'Tempted though I am to do as you

say, Clara darling, I fear it would make no difference,' Amelia said prosaically. 'A manor house and a number of tenant farmers to lord it over have already beguiled her into hitherto undreamed of airs and graces, no matter how uninhabitable we might try to make it! Even at Papa's funeral, the delight in her eyes at their unexpected rise in society was evident for all to see and there is nothing we can do to make it otherwise. Even if they decided not to make this their permanent dwelling, the manor and all its incumbent monies etc. now legally belong to them . . . and we are beholden to their benevolence in allowing us to stay here.'

'I shall hate it!' Clara declared with passion. 'I will feel like Fanny Price in Miss Austen's latest novel, *Mansfield Park*! We will be the poor relations indebted to their insincere charity! And the thought of that obnoxious brat of theirs lording it over us is intolerable in the extreme!'

'I expect Vernon was merely over-excited at being the only child present at Papa's funeral and consequently forgot his manners!'

'Fiddle-faddle! He was downright rude and neither his mother nor that French maid of hers made any move to correct him! He will run wild here!'

'Nevertheless, we will have to make the most of it,' Amelia reiterated. 'The only alternative is that we shall be completely homeless and thrown upon the charity of strangers. At least this way, we will have a roof over our heads and will still live among our known neighbours. Reverend and Mrs Peters assured me on Sunday that she hoped our friendship with them and our fellow-parishioners will continue unabated. As for those of our former friends who have abandoned us, how real was their friendship if they could cast us aside so easily?'

'Sophie Hughes dropped me like a hot potato as soon as Freddie dropped you,' Clara sighed. 'We'll forever be outcasts to them and their ilk! And I lost my only other close friend, Jane Dobson, when her father moved to Brighton to become headmaster of a new preparatory school there. No-one accepts us!'

'Ah! Now, I have some news for you there!' Amelia was glad to impart, recognising that they were in danger of wallowing in a fit of the blue-devils. 'Mrs Peters passed on the information that Colonel Usherwood's place is let at last, so we will once more have near neighbours.'

'As long as the local tittle-tattle doesn't put them off acknowledging us!' Clara said gloomily. 'Is it a family who have taken West Lodge?'

'Mrs Peters wasn't sure. No doubt we shall soon find out.'

With vases of fresh flowers to arrange and other last minute preparations to make, there was little time for further speculation. Mrs Tranter, anxious not to let the side down by any lack of culinary expertise, was busy in the kitchen, fretfully fussing over the menu that she and Amelia had agreed upon and driving Kate to distraction with her administrations.

At last, the butler, Gerard, scurried along the hallway.

'Potter says they're here, Miss Amelia! Just turned in at t'bottom o'driveway!' he imparted as he passed the two young women who were fussily tweaking the beautiful array of meadow flowers into place.

'Oh, my goodness! Are we ready?' Amelia asked, suddenly all aflutter.

'As ready as we'll ever be!' Clara sighed. 'Let's get it over with!'

They followed Gerard along the hall and waited while he drew back the huge bolts that fastened the stout oak door and turned the large key in its lock. The door swung silently on newly oiled hinges, letting bright rays of sunshine flood into the cool reception area.

A line of three carriages had already drawn to a halt as Amelia and Clara stepped on to the top level of the semi-circular stone steps and immediately looked at each other in consternation. The two rear carriages, sturdy hired town coaches by the look of them, were piled high with all sorts of trunks, boxes and odd-shaped packaging.

'Oh, my goodness! I think they've come to stay!' Clara gasped. 'I thought this visit was to talk things over and decide a time schedule!'

'So did I!' Amelia said faintly. She turned swiftly to the equally dumbfounded butler. 'Gerard, would you be so good as to tell Potter to direct the two rear carriages round to the yard. And . . . ' She swiftly looked around the reception hall, spying Kate industriously dusting the wainscoting. ' . . . Kate, dear, will you nip back to the kitchen and tell Mrs Tranter that the Forresters seem to be moving in lock, stock and barrel! Ask her to stop what she is doing and come to the hallway. Oh dear! I don't think I'm quite ready for this, Clara!'

'Take a few deep breaths, dearest.

That's what you always tell me!' Clara wisely advised, her own face slightly pale.

Amelia instantly complied with the suggestion and then patted her cheeks to bring some colour back into them. By the time she felt composed enough to step outside to greet the Forresters, the coachman of the leading carriage had leaped down from his seat and hurried to let down the step and open the carriage door.

Their cousin, Blake, was the first to step down. He was soberly dressed in beige breeches and gleaming top-boots, a brown double breasted coat, which Clara was sure had added padding at the shoulders, and a tall beaver hat upon his head. He stood and gazed about him with a satisfied air until he felt the sharp tap of his wife's hand upon his shoulder. If Amelia hadn't been feeling quite so tense, she might have smiled as he visibly jumped and hurriedly turned around to give his hand to his wife, Louisa, as she stepped delicately from the carriage.

She, too, gazed about with a proprietary air and a satisfied smile. Her high-crowned hat was trimmed to perfection with flowers and ostrich plumes and her dark green, heavily ornate carriage dress with ruched sleeves and a little winged ruff made her slight figure seem almost Junoesque.

Nine-year-old Vernon leaped down without assistance and immediately put both fists on to his hips as he surveyed Amelia and Clara who stood in ready welcome.

Amelia clutched her sister's hand and descended the three steps to greet the trio, though her heart had plummeted to her dainty shoes.

'Welcome to Moreton Manor, Cousin Blake and Louisa,' she smiled tremulously.

'And me!' Vernon demanded.

'Of course, and you, Vernon,' Amelia hastily amended.

'S-oo lovely to be here, Amelia, dear!' Cousin Louisa cooed, letting the tips of her fingers briefly touch Amelia's hand. 'As you can see, we're here to stay! You did get our communication to that effect, didn't you? It seemed so pointless to wait any longer! After all, we have given you your full mourning period! Such a shame about Ralph and then your poor father! But we said all that at the funeral, didn't we? I'm sure there's no need to go through it all again! It was obviously meant to be ... and you always knew Moreton Manor would never be yours, didn't you?'

Amelia felt her welcoming smile freeze on her face. 'Yes,' she replied briefly, dropping her hand. She moved on to offer her hand to Blake, who at least managed to convey a more sympathetic demeanour than his wife.

'It's so good of you to receive us so graciously, Amelia ... and you, also Clara. We hope ... er ... that you continue to regard the manor as your home.'

'For the time being!' Louisa added

29

sharply. 'There will, of course, be some changes that you will have to get used to!'

''Cos you won't be the lady of the manor any more!' Vernon's voice piped up. 'My mamma will!'

'Yes, well, we'll leave that for now, Vernon,' Blake said uncomfortably. 'Let's get inside before we discuss the future, shall we?'

Amelia was surprised how stricken she felt. She knew the words were the truth . . . but hearing them spoken so plainly completely un-nerved her. Her hand fluttered to her throat and she felt peculiarly light-headed.

Vernon's high-pitched voice startled her into reality.

'Where are all the servants?' he demanded. 'I thought you said the servants would line the steps to welcome us, Mamma! Make them come out!'

His comment wiped the smile from his mother's face and her lips tightened as she took in the bare steps.

'They are assembled inside,' Amelia

said hastily, hoping indeed that it was so. 'We hadn't had any communication from you to say you were coming permanently this visit . . . but, no matter. You are here now and we hope . . . ' She swallowed hard, her throat tightening on the words. 'We hope you will be as happy here as we have been. Now, do come inside. Once the servants have greeted you, Mrs Tranter will be wanting to serve afternoon tea. She has it all ready.'

'I hope you don't allow the servants to dictate times and places to you!' Louisa said sharply. 'I won't condone any slackness in my establishment, I assure you! Come now, Blake, give me your arm. You must lead me into our new home.'

With an apologetic moue at Amelia and Clara, Blake did as his wife bade him and gallantly offered her his arm and Louisa swept grandly up the three steps and through the doorway of the manor, with Vernon scampering after them.

Amelia and Clara exchanged rueful glances. Changes were already being made.

The next few hours were a torment to Amelia, Clara and all the servants. After sweeping past the hastily assembled servants with a haughty demeanour as they bowed or bobbed small curtsies, Louisa insisted on every door on the ground floor being flung open to enable her to make an initial assessment of what she had inherited.

'Everywhere is so dark!'

'What a dismal outlook! That will have to be changed!'

'Are you sure this room has been aired?'

'How can you bear so much panelling, Amelia? Really! It's like stepping back a whole century!'

'Would you like to see the kitchen?' Amelia asked, when all other rooms had been viewed.

Louisa brusquely waved her hand. 'No, thank you! I've seen enough for one day. I tell you, Blake, I was quite right to insist on moving in immediately!' She sighed dramatically. 'There is so much to do here, I swear we shall be busy for many months to come!'

Amelia felt the day was never going to end. A strained air pervaded over dinner . . . made no better by Louisa's comments when they were sitting together in the drawing room later in the evening.

'Really, Amelia! It doesn't surprise me that the manor is in such a deplorable state. You have been far too easygoing with the servants. It is a well-known fact that servants only respect their masters and mistresses if they are constantly reminded of their lowly place in society! You will notice that I never say, 'please' or 'thank you' to a servant! It is their job and their duty to do our bidding and they must not be allowed to forget it!'

Amelia felt her cheeks enflame as she struggled to retain her composure, as this wasn't the first of such comments.

'I beg to differ, Louisa. I have always

found that a display of consideration and appreciation goes a long way towards maintaining a harmonious relationship with the household staff.'

Louisa's eyebrows almost disappeared into her hair. 'Harmonious relationship!' she echoed. 'They must do as they are told or leave their employment! I shall be making that very clear at the outset! Now, dear, you mustn't be angry with me for saying so. I believe in being open about these things. However, you were quite young when your poor mama died — sixteen or so, weren't you? Barely younger than Clara is now . . . and you wouldn't put the running of the house into her hands, would you?'

She held up her hand to cut off the protest that Amelia was about to make.

'Now, no more dissent. You have done your best and we shall leave it at that. I will make an inspection of the kitchen at eleven o'clock tomorrow morning. Be so good as to inform Cook, and also inform her that Mr

Forrester rises early and has need of an early breakfast. He holds an important position with the government, you know, and will frequently remain in town for a number of days at a time. Vernon, the dear boy rises at about nine o'clock and will eat breakfast in the schoolroom with his tutor. And I will partake of a light breakfast at ten o'clock . . . but my maid, Mathilde, will oversee that.

'There, now! I think we have begun very nicely, don't you? And tomorrow, you and I must have a little heart-to-heart, Amelia. But now, you must bid me goodnight. As it has been a busy day for us all and I think we shall all benefit from a good night's sleep.'

Amelia and Clara were filled with a mixture of anger, resentment and frustration when they retired to their rooms and sleep did not come easily. Amelia feared that many sweeping changes would be made before they settled into a harmonious household . . . and the kitchen inspection the following day did nothing to allay her fears.

By the time it was over, Kate was sobbing on a kitchen stool and Mrs Tranter had avowed she would have left immediately except it was unthinkable that she would leave her two young ladies alone in the care of 'that bracket-faced vixen'!

Luncheon was a stilted affair and when it had been cleared away, Clara was bidden to keep an eye on Vernon while he explored the garden. Aware of Amelia's foreboding about the promised tête-á-tête, she reluctantly agreed.

Louisa led the way into the sitting-room, a snug and homely room that had hosted many a happy afternoon or evening's companionship for the Havertons, and seated herself on the sofa. She patted the place at her side.

'Come and sit next to me, Amelia, so that we can speak more easily.'

She waited until Amelia had done so and then reached over and patted her hand. 'I am about to do some plain speaking but I see no reason to delay saying what must be said. In fact, you are an intelligent young woman and I dare say you must already be thinking along similar lines!'

Amelia looked at her uncomprehendingly.

'I'm not sure,' she faltered. 'Both Clara and I are sensible enough to know that a lot of compromise must be made and I hope we are gracious enough not to mind overmuch when you change things to your own liking. Indeed, I expect we shall find ourselves greatly pleased, for we know you have greater experience than we have and have been into many fine houses in London.'

'I am sure you are right. I have so many fine plans that I hardly know where to begin. But that is not what I am alluding to. Oh, dear! I know it must all be very hard for you and Clara ... but we find ourselves in this awkward situation and so we have to make the best of it. This has been your home throughout your lifetime and now it is mine. As I said yesterday, you are welcome to stay here for the time being but let us hope that it is not too long before you are planning to leave.'

'Leave?' Amelia echoed. 'But we have nowhere to go . . . or we would have gone long before now. We have no other relations and, until we come of age, no money to enable us to set ourselves up somewhere! Nor have we had any training to enable us to make our own way in the world. I cannot think . . . '

She looked blankly at her cousin-by-marriage.

Louise trilled with laughter. 'Silly goose! Of course I am not suggesting that you go out and earn your own living — though I have no doubt that you would find yourself capable of something, if it were ever to come to that! No, I am talking of marriage! As I see it, now that your mourning period is over, the best possible solution to our domestic problem will be for you to make an advantageous match as quickly as possible!'

Amelia stared at Louisa in dismay, her cheeks burning with embarrassment.

'I . . . I have n . . . no thoughts of getting married,' she faltered. 'Indeed, I doubt whether any so-called 'advantageous match' could be made for either me or my sister! You must realise that when Ralph . . . the insinuations that were cast about . . . the taint of scandal . . . '

She found she was unable to form complete sentences, so great was her distress, and she struggled to compose herself. 'I'm afraid that marriage is completely out of the question!'

'Nonsense! What other position is there for a woman of your upbringing apart from that of a wife? A governess, maybe, or a lady's maid? Possibly . . . but, more likely you would end up a drudge in some household or other. Is that what you want? No, I thought not.'

Louisa patted Amelia's hand again. 'Now, don't look so despondent, I am

39

sure that many a man may be persuaded to come up to scratch! You have passable looks and a dowry of three thousand pounds. Not a great sum, to be sure, but better than nothing! As for the scandal, I am sure it has died down already. Why, I have heard practically nothing about it for six months at least!'

Amelia shook her head. 'The stain will never go away. You must know that Freddie Hughes lost no time in crying off, even though we had an 'understanding'. He couldn't wait to sever all connections!'

Louisa waved her hand dismissively. 'I wasn't thinking of anyone so well connected, my dear. That is now completely out of your reach . . . but I am sure we'll find someone to marry you. Anyone will do! After all, what other hope have you?'

# 3

Amelia stared at Louisa in anguish. 'But I don't wish to marry just anyone! I would prefer to marry for love. But, failing that, at least with liking and respect. The same for Clara. I had hoped that we could stay here until I come of age. We would live very quietly. We wouldn't be much of a burden to you.'

'No, no. That wouldn't do,' Louisa said sharply. 'People would always point the finger at us all. Mr Forrester and I need a completely new start . . . and to re-establish connections with the Hughes at the Hall and to become acquainted with the new residents at West Lodge. We have Vernon's future to think about, you must realise. I know it is a few years away yet, but, one day, he'll want to bring a bride to this house. Just think how it would seem if the daughters of the previous incumbent still lived here!'

'Obviously, much worse than if you had thrown us out into the street!' Amelia said bitterly. She was immediately ashamed of her resort to sarcasm. 'I'm sorry. That was remiss of me. I do understand that we present a difficult situation. But, please, if we may remain here until I come of age, I am sure that something will present itself to enable me to support both myself and Clara by some modest means until our . . . situation . . . improves in some way.'

Louisa sighed. 'I feel you are too optimistic by far on that score! But, we shall see. I have no wish to force you into something you find quite abhorrent, so we shall say no more for the moment. However, that doesn't mean that you can forget what I have said! To my mind, the sooner it is sorted the better and don't forget, as a 'married' sister, you will have a far greater chance of settling Clara advantageously! Think about it, my dear!'

Over the next few days, Amelia did little else than think about it. Not wanting to make Clara feel as wretched as herself, she told her only that Louisa had discussed various options open to them for their future, such as marriage or some other vague means of support.

'But not until I come of age,' she hastened to assure Clara at her look of alarm. 'And that is still some months away!'

The joining of the two households brought a number of problems of its own, not least among the servants. Ellis, Blake's valet considered himself of greater importance than the 'countrified' Gerard, who, as butler, was used to taking his place at the head of the kitchen table. And Mathilde, Louisa's French maid, refused to eat in the kitchen at all. She merely flounced in to issue sharp orders as to the needs of her mistress in her accented voice and ordered Kate to make up a tray for her to eat in solitary style upstairs.

After a few days of frequent inspections of the kitchen and constant haranguing of the maids at their work, Louisa was satisfied that she had the servants' measure . . . and they hers!

'You will see how much better the house is run now that the servants are aware that they must be alert to the needs of the family at all times,' Louisa pointed out to Amelia.

Amelia forbore to tell her of the many ruffles she had been forced to smooth in the aftermath of Louisa's vigilance and the threats of 'walking out' that she had diverted. Louisa now devoted most of her time to discussing her plans for the many alterations with a house designer she had hired for this purpose and in making visits to town to select fabrics and wall-coverings.

Thankfully, Vernon was considered to be the responsibility of Mr Smithers, his somewhat elderly tutor, for the duration of the mornings and such afternoon as Louisa felt the need.

Amelia subsequently found that more

and more of the general overseeing of the running of the house fell upon her shoulders. It was no hardship to her as this had been her unofficial role since her mother had died four years previously. The only difference was that she had to report daily to Louisa with carefully worded suggestions rather than ideas already decided, but she felt that she was in some measure earning her keep and enjoyed the responsibility, secretly hoping that it would solve the problem over what was to become of their future.

Clara busied herself with her drawing, stitching and her accomplished playing of the pianoforte . . . her life only really changing when she had perforce to take charge of Vernon, for the odd half hour in order to restrain him from getting into mischief.

As the second week slipped away, Louisa fretted that none of the society people of the area had deigned to visit or leave their cards and Amelia was greatly embarrassed when Louisa forcibly approached the Hughes family as they departed from the village church after morning service on the second Sunday since their arrival.

' . . . for I was uncertain if you knew of our presence at Moreton Manor,' Amelia heard Louisa say.

Amelia froze and wished only to blend among the gravestones, drawing Clara aside with her, as Mrs Hughes looked down her aristocratic nose, obviously highly affronted by Louisa's forwardness and said coldly. 'No, I'm afraid we didn't.'

Louisa should have taken the snub for what it was and retired from the scene with what grace she could muster, but she pressed on, desperately trying to prolong the conversation.

'I am holding an afternoon tea party a week on Wednesday and I would be honoured by your presence.'

'I doubt we will be at home on that day,' Mrs Hughes said in dismissive tones. 'Good day.'

Louisa's face flamed. 'Well, really!' she said to no-one in particular as the

Hughes family departed through the lyche gate with their heads held high.

Amelia took pity on her and moved forward to rejoin her.

'Don't take it personally,' she commiserated. 'I'm afraid it's your family connection to us that made Mrs Hughes cut you like that. She is the mother of the man I was engaged to.'

'I am fully aware of who she is!' Louisa said coldly. 'Now, isn't this what I spoke to you about the other day? Your presence here will forever sour any hope of a relationship with the Hughes.'

Amelia bit back the distress Louisa's words caused. She knew it was true, but the words expressed so openly were very hurtful. She spotted Mr and Mrs Dewberry, the schoolmaster and his wife, emerging from the porch and touched Louisa's arm. 'Why don't you invite Mrs Dewberry to tea with you, Louisa? I am sure she will be only too happy to come along.'

Louisa looked scandalised. 'The schoolmaster's wife? Why on earth would I invite her to partake of tea with me? I doubt she will be able to influence society for me. No, my dear. The only way to progress socially is to aim higher than one's own social standing.' She glanced about her at the now dwindling churchgoers. 'Our other new neighbours weren't here, were they? They must have money and influence or they wouldn't be able to afford to rent West Lodge. That's the way I need to go. Come along into the carriage, Vernon. Maybe you two girls should walk home. The exercise will be good for you!'

'Huh! More like she hopes we won't be associated with her!' Clara hissed once Louisa was out of earshot.

'Hush, dearest . . . or we make ourselves to be of the same cut. Whatever else we sink to, we can keep our self respect.'

A few days later, a short note was hand-delivered to the manor. Louisa was resting upstairs and it was Amelia who took it from Gerard's hand.

'I think it's the reply from the Davenports, the new tenants of West Lodge,' she told Clara. 'Louisa will be overjoyed!'

It was only as Amelia was dressing for dinner that she remembered that the note lay unopened on the hall table. She hurried downstairs to retrieve it and took it to Louisa's dressing room, knowing she would want to read it immediately.

Louisa seized upon it with great delight.

Her face fell, however, as she tore the note open and began to read. '*Mr Davenport regrets that he does not intend to be at home to society in the foreseeable future!*' she quoted bitterly. 'The shame of your brother's conduct is going to blight us for the rest of our lives!'

Amelia felt outraged. 'Ralph did nothing to be ashamed of!' she declared quietly. 'He carried the blame for someone else's action . . . and if there were any way to prove his innocence, I would do it! As it is, we carry his memory with love and I would appreciate it if you forbore to cast a slur upon his name every time he is mentioned.'

'It's all very well for you to speak thus, Amelia,' Louisa countered, 'but I have Vernon's future to think about. It isn't fair to him to have to carry someone else's burden of shame like this!'

'You were keen to step into Ralph's inheritance!' Amelia pointed out coldly. 'It seems, in this case, that the one goes with other.'

'Made worse by the fact that we are sheltering the traitor's sisters!' Louisa spat back. 'I'm sorry, Amelia, but I must say it again, the sooner you and Clara settle yourselves somewhere else, the better it will be for all concerned! We have no wish to put you and Clara out upon the streets . . . but I'll give you shelter until you come of age and no longer! And that is very generous of us under the circumstances.'

Amelia's throat felt constricted and speech was impossible. This ultimatum had been uttered before but never so harshly. She had kept hoping that something would happen to make it less painful. Suddenly, on top of Louisa's unkind words about Ralph, it was too much to bear.

'I . . . Oh! Excuse me! I cannot . . .' and, with her fingers spread across her trembling lips, she hurried from the room. Where should she go? She had no wish to speak of what had taken place with Clara whilst she was feeling so upset. Neither could she bear to present herself at the dinner table and act as if nothing untoward had happened.

She ran down the stairs, turned into the library and hurried over to the full-length windows, thankful that they opened easily. It was a warm, balmy evening and she hurried across the terrace and the tended lawn, making for the cover of the small orchard that bordered their land. There was an old summerhouse on its outer edge that the three of them had used as a den in their childhood days and would now offer the solitude she needed.

Its door was broken and hung awkwardly on its hinges but it swung open under the pressure of her hand. The seats were worn and, in the gloom of the twilight hour, they looked unsafe to sit upon and Amelia turned about and sat forlornly on the doorstep, her eyes blurred by the tears that now fell freely down her cheeks.

As her tears lessened, her common-sense reasserted itself and she thought of the money that was to be hers in a few months' time. Surely it would buy a modest place somewhere? But, what would they live on? The thought of becoming a governess horrified her. She had little experience of children and, if Vernon was anything to go by, little empathy.

She supposed she could become some sort of lady's maid, though they had never entered much into society and knew little of its ways. A housekeeper, then? That was where her natural talent lay, of that she was sure. But, how to find a position? Would Mrs Peters be able to advise her?

Calmed by her rational thinking, Amelia became more aware of her surroundings. The light had faded more and she knew she ought to be returning to the house. A sudden crashing in the undergrowth not far away from her caused a sense of alarm and, as she rose to her feet, she heard a ghastly howl of pain erupt through the bushes. Her hand clutched at her throat and she hovered hesitantly. What was it? What should she do?

Softer yelps of pain and whimpering calmed her fears. It was an animal in pain, of that, she was sure. She knew that some landowners laid traps in their woodlands to deter intruders but her father had never allowed such on his land. But, the orchard bordered woodland that was a sort of no-man's land between their land and that of Colonel Usherwood of West Lodge. He had long since given up personal supervision of his land and, since going to live with relatives a few years ago, his land had been left neglected. The new tenant had only just taken up residence there. Had poachers got in and laid traps?

Her mind now certain of what had happened, Amelia forgot her earlier fear and began to hurry forward through the unkempt shrubs and bushes, drawing ever nearer to the faint sounds of the animal's whimpering. Her dress was torn and her hands scratched by the time she parted the last tangle of brambles and other branches.

Through the gloom, she could just make out the form of a large dog lying on the ground in front of her. One of its rear legs was caught between the cruel jaws of a metal trap, its flesh torn and bloody from the dog's frantic efforts to free itself.

'Oh! You poor dog!' she gasped, dropping to her knees at the dog's side.

The dog growled, baring its teeth and Amelia sat back on her heels a little.

'It's all right. I won't hurt you,' she

said soothingly. 'Lie still, there's a good boy.' She laid her hand on its back and after initially flinching at her touch, the animal lay still, though tense beneath her hand. She continued to make soothing noises, gently stroking the dog's flank, averting her eyes from the ghastly sight of its mangled hind leg.

What on earth was she to do? She didn't feel she could leave the animal, yet how else was she to get help? Who was his owner? Was it the new tenant of West Lodge? That was the most obvious answer. She stood up and tried to prise open the metal jaws that held the dog's leg in their unrelenting grip but she felt not the slightest movement.

'I can't help you,' she whispered, dropping down again. 'I'll have to leave you to get help.'

The dog suddenly let out a high-pitched whimper. Afraid that she had accidentally hurt him, she glanced at his hindquarters and was surprised to see that he was making feeble attempts to wag his tail. In the stillness of the moment, she became aware that a male voice was calling.

'Russ! Here, boy! Here, boy!'

Amelia scrambled to her feet and peered in the direction of the calling voice.

'Here! He's over here! Oh, do hurry! He's badly hurt!'

'Where are you? Keeping calling to me!' the male voice ordered, coming closer with each syllable.

Amelia dropped back down beside the wounded animal, stroking him reassuringly and called repeatedly, 'Here! Here! Over here!' until the sounds of someone hastily forcing his way through the thick shrubbery and undergrowth came close at hand.

As the man emerged into sight, Amelia could tell he was tall and of slender build, though no weakling. In the faded light of the shrubbery she could tell he was of dark complexion. His hand, which brushed hers as he ran it experimentally down the dog's flank, felt firm and strong. He grasped her hand, lifting it from the dog's back.

'You've done well to keep him calm,' he praised. He shifted his position and swiftly assessed the metal trap, using his hands to assist his eyes. 'If I can force it open a little, do you think you will be able to pull his leg free?' he asked abruptly.

'Yes . . . but it is very strong. I tried it myself.

He laughed, a little harshly. 'You would be a rare woman if you had succeeded! Are you ready?'

Amelia felt the man's hands guiding hers into place.

'There . . . and there,' he said. 'Be ready to do it swiftly when I say . . . but, if in any doubt, you must swiftly pull your right hand away.' His voice was quiet but firm. 'Do not risk getting it caught! I love my dog . . . but I won't have him the cause of a severed hand! Do you understand?'

Amelia swallowed hard. She understood only too well!

'Yes,' she whispered.

He stood up and Amelia sensed him bracing himself. She felt his leg tense against her shoulder and heard him grunt, 'Now!'

Amelia swiftly eased the broken limb clear of the wicked teeth and pulled it clear with her left hand. The dog yelped and the man cursed as he released his hands and leaped aside. He cursed again.

'Are you all right?' Amelia gasped.

The man laughed harshly. 'It's caught my sleeve! No matter!' He wrenched it clear and then dropped to her side again, stroking the dog's back. 'I need to get him home but I can't risk him walking on this shattered leg. It will never mend if it gets further damaged. Here! Hold my coat!'

He swiftly shrugged off his coat and handed it to Amelia and then ripped open the buttons of his shirt and tore it from his back. His bare flesh gleamed against the darkness around them and Amelia hoped he didn't hear the tiny intake of breath that escaped her lips.

She felt an awareness of something stirring deep within her as the man used his teeth and his hands to tear the shirt into strips and swiftly wrap them around the dog's bleeding leg.

In spite of the poor light, Amelia realised with a stab of awareness that she knew whom he was. He was the horseman who had chased away the men who had attacked her and Clara when they were blackberrying and, of course, Russ was the large dog that had accompanied him.

# 4

Amelia remembered that she had felt a little alarmed by his appearance on that earlier occasion but now she felt perfectly safe with him. Any man who vowed his love for his dog would cause her no harm, she reasoned.

'I must now lift him on to my shoulders,' she realised the man was saying, interrupting her reverie. 'Don't be alarmed when he yelps.'

'Do you want to put your coat on first?'

'No. Why ruin it more than it is already? If you will be so good as to carry it for me ... ' He left the sentence unfinished as he turned back to his log. 'Stand, boy!' he ordered.

The dog struggled to his feet and the man leaned over him. With a swift heave and twist ... and the promised yelp of pain from the dog ... he had the dog straddled across his bare shoulders.

'Right!' Follow me! I must get him home as quickly as I can.'

With no more ado, the man set off at a fast loping run, his back bowed under his weight of his dog. Amelia obediently followed, not even considering excusing herself and returning home.

It took them ten minutes or more to clear the woodland and Amelia knew they were heading in the direction of West Lodge. So, she was right. This was Mr Davenport, the new tenant.

As they crossed a meadow, she knew she was dropping further behind but continued to follow in Mr Davenport's wake, his coat clutched in her arms. Suddenly, she heard male voices ahead and saw lanterns swinging, followed by loud exclamations . . . and, belatedly, it seemed, a lantern swung in her direction and came towards her.

A man's gruff voice asked, 'You all right, miss?'

'Yes, thank you,' Amelia replied.

She made better headway following the lantern and it wasn't long before they were entering the West Lodge grounds from the rear and heading towards the stable and outbuildings.

The dog was already lying on a rough blanket of some sort and Mr Davenport was kneeling at his side, carefully unwrapping his improvised bandages. Another man brought a bowl of water and Mr Davenport began to carefully sponge the dog's shattered limb. He seemed to know what he was doing and the other three men around him assisted almost wordlessly, as if they were used to doing so. A younger man hovered in the background, but, although he showed signs at the dog's condition, he didn't actively co-operate with the others.

There was a murmured discussion among the older men, seemingly over whether or not the leg could be saved, and the consensus of opinion was that it was worth trying. Splints were fashioned and bandaged around the limb and, eventually, the task was complete.

Only then did Mr Davenport get to his feet and arch his back. It still bore the blood of his dog and other marks that Amelia realised were scars from some fairly recent wounds. She shivered at the sight and the slight sound she made caused Mr Davenport to swing around and face her. The look of surprise on his face was almost comical and Amelia realised that he had forgotten she was there.

'I beg your pardon,' he apologised straight away. 'You must think me the most ill-mannered of men!'

'Your mind was on more urgent matters,' Amelia concurred, as she handed him his coat. 'And rightly so. You seem to have made a proficient job of fixing your dog's leg.'

'Only time will tell just how proficient,' he agreed, shrugging his arms into the sleeves of his coat. 'The next few days ... hours, even ... However ... ' He seemed to make a conscious effort to pull his thoughts together. 'I really must thank you for your part in all this. Your cool presence of mind; your ready acceptance of what was needed to be done. Many a young lady would have fainted or had histrionics at far less a situation, and I don't even know your name — yet, I feel we have met somewhere . . . ?'

'My sister and I were picking blackberries a week or so ago,' Amelia reminded him, sensing a sudden awkwardness in the atmosphere. ' . . . and were set upon by two ruffians . . . you must have witnessed it somehow and came to our assistance.'

Mr Davenport laughed. 'So I did! Belatedly, it seemed to me later . . . as you had already dispersed the 'ruffians' with your stick and your admirable courage!'

Amelia wasn't sure, but it seemed to her that her use of the word 'ruffians' caused him some amusement and that he had deliberately re-used it himself.

'And, please, don't look so indignant,' Mr Davenport pleaded, as if he had read her thoughts. 'I am truly full of admiration for your presence of mind and courage on both occasions. Any levity implied by my words was directed at myself. I am unused to being of superfluous use to someone as . . . ' He hesitated, as if unsure which words to use that would cause the least offence.

Amelia inwardly chuckled at his obvious dilemma.

'Sweetly feminine?' he tried, his eyes also lit by amusement. 'You'll have to help me out, I'm afraid! I've been too long on the Peninsular battlefields to be able to speak fine words to a lady such as yourself.'

Amelia laughed, feeling utterly in rapport with him, marvelling that it should be so on so slight an acquaintance. Or rather, on no acquaintance, if the truth be told.

'Sir, I have no patience with silly women who simper and smile and expect men to flatter them at every moment. Respect and admiration should be earned before it can be sincerely given!'

'Well, you have earned both, in my

opinion, and I don't even know your name, nor how you came to be so appropriately on hand.' He self-consciously wiped his palm against his trousers and held it out towards Amelia. 'My name is Edward Davenport, Ned to my friends and I have recently taken West Lodge as my temporary residence until . . . until I am sorted out. I am in the process of resigning my commission.'

Amelia savoured his name as she took hold of his outstretched hand. Ned. 'I thought that must be your name,' she acknowledged ingenuously. 'My family lives next door to you, in the manor house. At least, we did until our brother died . . . in the war . . . and then Papa died. And, now . . . oh, dear . . . but you don't want to hear all this. It is of no account.'

Her voice broke and she swallowed hard and strived to prevent any tiresome tears from falling. Suddenly, however, all the upsets and fears of the past year, months and weeks came back in to prominence and she felt her outer composure in danger of slipping away. She realised that Ned was still holding her hand and was looking intently into her eyes. She tried to withdraw her hand but he held it firmly.

'It is 'of account' to you,' he acknowledged, 'and I can see that it distresses you, and that tells me the possible reason why you were outside at such an unconventional hour. So, although it is no business of mine, I feel, in some way, that our lives have crossed for a purpose.'

He studied her face for some moments, seeing genuine distress blurring the courage and bravery that he had instinctively sensed there previously. He felt an overwhelming desire to wrap her in his arms and tell her that she needn't worry any more.

But, just as that thought whispered across his mind, the rational part of him rebutted his cavalier instinct. He was in no position to help her, not with any permanence.

So, he didn't utter any platitudes.

Instead, he gently raised her fingers to her lips, knowing that the shaft of fire that coursed through him, also coursed through her. And then he tucked her hand on to his arm and held it there.

He laughed ruefully. 'You must think me the most ungentlemanly person you have ever had the misfortune to meet! Let us go inside and I will see that some refreshment is served to you whilst I make myself more presentable. And then, I will escort you home. Whatever your problems are, I am sure your presence will have been missed and there will be much anxiety about your whereabouts.'

They went in through a side entrance and she could tell at once that little had been done to the Lodge since the Colonel's days there had ended. But, of course, his household hadn't had time to be established yet. They had barely been in residence for a week.

As if suddenly aware of the short-comings of his home, Ned spread his arm in a deprecatory manner. 'I am sorry, I can't offer you much comfort,' he apologised. 'As you have probably noticed, we are not yet fully operational.'

'Have you no housekeeper?' Amelia asked.

'Not yet, though I expect I shall need to acquire one. We are a bachelor household, as you have probably realised.'

'Yes. I'm afraid Cousin Louisa was very disappointed by your note. She had hoped to make her way in society riding on your coat-tails, I'm afraid.'

He raised an eyebrow. 'Ah, yes. Mrs Forrester. And she is . . . ?'

'My cousin, Blake's wife. They are the ones who now own the manor. It was entailed, you know.'

'Ah, I see. And you have no brothers?'

'Not since Ralph died last year . . . and Papa died shortly afterwards, from the shock, I suppose.'

'Ralph? You had a brother called Ralph? I'm sorry. It's very remiss of me, but I still don't know your name.'

'Amelia Haverton. There's just me and my younger sister, Clara. She is sixteen and is less prepared than I am to make her way in the world. But Louisa has said she will give us no longer than when I come of age in a few months' time.' She didn't know why she was sharing the intimate details of her problem with him.

'I'm sorry,' she apologised. 'I shouldn't be burdening you with all this. You are newly arrived and, no doubt, have problems of your own. Maybe, if you have a carriage, you could ask for it to be sent round and I will return home.' She suddenly realised that his expression had altered and wondered the reason. 'What is it? Why are you looking at me like that? Have I said something out of place?'

He shook his head. 'Your brother, you said his name was Ralph? Ralph Haverton?'

'Yes. What of it?' Her voice was suddenly sharp. He must have heard the rumours of disgrace and would now express his condemnation!

But Ned's voice sounded more shocked than condemnatory when he spoke. 'I know him . . . knew him, since you say he has died. I'm sorry. I liked him. We got on well together. I knew he lived somewhere around here.'

He paused and then reached out and took hold of her hand. 'I'm sorry. You must think me a blundering fool. You are still mourning him and I am resurrecting old wounds. Forgive me.'

Amelia had glanced down in her distress and expectation of hearing her brother's name defiled but now she raised her eyes again and saw only compassion in Ned's eyes.

'It is over a year and we are out of mourning, but you are right. I will mourn his death forever. He was a good brother and we miss him, and not only because his death means we must lose our home. But you were not to know . . . and it is good to hear someone . . .' She was going to say 'who speaks well of him,' but she could not bear to have to explain the circumstances surrounding the time of Ralph's death and so altered her words to, ' . . . who knew him . . . and liked him.'

'I should think everyone who knew him, liked him,' Ned countered, 'and I as exceedingly sorry that he is no longer alive. If it doesn't distress you, we will talk more of him at another time.'

A discreet knock at the door heralded the entrance of a soberly dressed man.

'Good man, Payling,' Ned greeted his appearance. 'Will you bring a tray of refreshment for Miss Haverton? You will have heard from the others how she helped me discover poor Russ and assisted most admirably in helping to free him.'

'Yes, sir,' Payling murmured. 'We have some cold meats, bread and cheese . . . and some large plums gathered from the orchard only this afternoon.'

When Payling withdrew, Ned excused himself and went upstairs to wash and change and Amelia sank back against the sofa. How amazing that their new neighbour had known Ralph, and had implied that they were more than mere acquaintances.

Her face clouded. Would he still speak of him with admiration when he heard the sordid gossip? She had better speak of it herself before someone else did, but not tonight. She had had enough upset to cope with for one day. And yet her time spent with Ned Davenport had dispelled the distress Louisa had caused.

She felt a warm contentment at the thought of him. He displayed none of the insincere flattery that abounded in society. In fact, his manner, however unconventional, had been perfectly courteous. She also realised with a start that she had hardly noticed the scar that ran down his right cheek, in spite of the fact that it had caused her some apprehension on their first meeting.

When Payling brought a plate of cold meats and a dish of red plums on a serviceable tray a few moments later, Amelia tucked into the food with relish. She laughingly excused her appetite when Ned reappeared, simply, though elegantly, attired in beige ankle-length trousers and a dark green cut-away coat. They conversed of mundane matters while they shared the dish of plums and Amelia felt as though they had known each other for years. In spite of that, she was happy when Payling announced that the carriage was at the front entrance.

Later, she couldn't recall what they had talked about during the short journey, except that the conversation had been natural and convivial . . . and that it had left her totally unprepared for the furore she caused when her return home was announced in the drawing room.

'You have been where?' Louisa asked, her eyebrows arched with incredulity. 'Have you no idea of the anxiety you have caused? And all the while you have been behaving no better than a common hussy!'

Amelia's face whitened with shock. 'Louisa! Nothing improper occurred! I found Mr Davenport's dog injured. I helped to free him. Nothing was planned and Mr Davenport was most courteous.'

She half-turned to indicate Ned's presence behind her but a partially stifled gasp from Louisa halted her movement. The look of revulsion on Louisa's face shocked her.

'What is it, Louisa?'

Her words died away. She knew what the matter was . . . and her knowledge was reinforced when she turned to see the tightness around Ned's mouth. She instantly knew that Louisa wasn't the first insensitive person to react thus at the sight of his scar and she cast a compassionate glance towards him, using his given name without thought.

'Ned!'

He held out his hand, palm forward, to deter her instinctive movement to his side as he faced Louisa and made a curt bow.

'I must apologise, Ma'am, for my thoughtlessness in detaining Miss Haverton, but I can assure you that no impropriety occurred. My men were in attendance the whole time and I must commend Miss Haverton for her remarkable courage.'

Louisa drew herself upright. 'Your apology is all very well, Mr Davenport,' she said coldly, 'but we know nothing about you. You must realise that my ward's reputation has been severely compromised by this day's mischief. You say your men were in attendance — but did you think to provide a female chaperone for Miss Haverton?'

'Why, no! My household is an all-male establishment. I haven't yet engaged any female staff.'

Amelia saw a flicker of calculation cross Louisa's face but, even so, she was unprepared for her next words.

'Then your action has done Miss Haverton grievous harm today, Mr Davenport. In the absence of my husband, I must take it upon myself to demand satisfaction for her honour . . . and the only way to avoid a scandal is for you to offer for Miss Haverton's hand in marriage!'

# 5

Amelia gasped with shock. 'Don't be ridiculous, Louisa! There is no scandal, except in your own mind . . . '

She flung a defiant glance towards Ned. His expression was unreadable but she felt she detected a mixture of shock and extreme distaste — and could she blame him! How could Louisa humiliate her so? Why, he might even think it had all been planned and that she had conspired to ensnare him!

' . . . and there is no need for any redress. Mr Davenport is not to be coerced into making me an offer. In fact, if he does so, I shall immediately refuse him!'

Amelia sensed that Ned's demeanour relaxed somewhat and wondered if indeed he was in no position to offer marriage whatever her decision. 'Besides,' she continued, wrathfully facing Louisa, 'for all you know, Mr Davenport might already be married . . . with a brood of children around his ankles.'

She glanced back at Ned, wondering if he would admit to such dependents and was sure she saw a momentary flicker of amusement in his eyes . . . but, the next moment, his eyes were impassive.

'And are you thus already encumbered, Mr Davenport?' Louisa asked coldly.

Ned bowed slightly in her direction.

'No, ma'am. I am not.'

'And what of your estate? Have you the means to support a wife?'

'Louisa!' Amelia implored, her face red with embarrassment. 'Don't answer her!' she entreated Ned.

He momentarily glanced her way, his right eyebrow slightly raised, but instantly returned to face Louisa.

'I have my soldier's pay and pension,' he admitted. 'I have served in the army since my late teens and have accrued a small amount of money.'

'Then, you will do very well indeed!' Louisa snapped. 'We will expect you to call upon Mr Forrester in the morning! You may go!'

Without even glancing at Amelia, Ned bowed stiffly in Louisa's direction — then turned abruptly on his heels and left the room.

Amelia made as if to run after him, to implore him to take no notice of Louisa's ridiculous scheme, for that is what it was. Even if Ned had been a travelling player or vagabond, Louisa would have made the same insistence as long as he could take her off her hands.

However, Louisa's sharp, 'Stay here!' made her hesitate and by the time she had made recovery and darted into the hallway, Gerard had already closed the front door upon their departed visitor.

Totally humiliated, she returned to the drawing room. Louisa was now seated on the sofa with a satisfied smile upon her lips. Amelia felt a wave of anger wash over her.

'How could you humiliate me so, Louisa?' she demanded bitterly. 'Mr Davenport had shown me nothing but respect. You had no right to treat him shamefully!'

'I have every right, Amelia. He wilfully compromised you and put our whole family at risk of further scandal. It is you who has acted shamefully by aiding and abetting him! No well brought-up girl would enter a bachelor establishment with or without adequate chaperonage. What will our neighbours think of it? The Hughes? The Peters, even?'

'And who will tell them?' Amelia demanded scornfully.

'These things have a way of getting out,' Louisa said lightly. 'Now, stop being a silly girl and consider the advantages of the situation. You will now be able to make a respectable marriage, maybe not of the best in society, but well enough. After all, you are hardly a diamond of the first water yourself and you only had the one offer from Freddie Hughes after your season in London!'

'I only wanted the one offer,' Amelia pointed out quietly. 'I imagined myself in love with Freddie and he with me. I soon realised how naïve I had been! At the first whiff of scandal, he soon made himself scarce!'

'One can hardly blame him, dear! But, enough of him! There are more fish in the sea and Mr Davenport bears himself well. He could be regarded as being quite handsome but for that hideous scar. He might not be as plump in the pocket as you might wish, but I imagine you will manage quite well between you, especially since you have lived all your life in this back-water of a place and have no pretensions towards moving amongst the upper circles.

'Now, why don't you retire to your room for the night? Wash your face in rose water before you go to bed and dream about your coming nuptials! With any luck we should have you married before winter is upon us.'

Amelia listened in growing incredulity. Did Louisa truly expect her to go along with her harebrained scheme? Looking at her, Amelia really believed she did. Well, she would have to think again!

'I can only hope my cousin, Blake, talks some sense into you, Louisa,' she said as calmly as she could. 'Goodnight.'

She had not long been in her room when she heard some scratching at the door and her sister, Clara, slipped into the room.

'Where have you been?' Clara demanded. 'There was such a to-do! Louisa was having histrionics and Vernon declared that you had thrown yourself into the river until I reminded him that it is no more than six inches deep. Louisa was demanding that Gerard hightail it to town to fetch Blake home but, when she saw the carriage turning into the drive she sent me upstairs. Who was it who brought you home? I couldn't see him properly but he seemed very tall and presentably dressed.'

'To answer your last question first, he is our new neighbour, Mr Davenport — Ned, to his friends, he said and, at the time, I felt he meant me . . . but, after Louisa's machinations have been made known, he will more than likely flee the country and never return!'

With Clara wrapped up in the eiderdown from Amelia's bed, Amelia proceeded to tell her sister all that had happened, without confiding the way her heart pounded and fluttered in Mr Davenport's presence. That information was best kept to herself since nothing could ever come of it. She must reconcile herself to the fact that she would have to find some way to support both herself and her sister and hope that Clara had more good fortune than herself.

The next morning she had hoped for a quiet breakfast, with just herself and Clara but Louisa made a rare appearance and scolded her for her wan appearance.

'I declare no man worth his salt

would offer for such an insipid creature!' she reprimanded. 'Now pinch your cheeks to bring some colour into them and I have decided that Mathilde will help you dress and do your hair. After all, in spite of the circumstances, we mustn't make a cheapskate out of this proposal. Now, practise lowering your eyes and looking up through your lashes likes so . . . and you will have Mr Davenport rushing to the altar before we have time to count to ten!'

Amelia refused to be jollied out of her low spirit but, as soon as breakfast was over, she dutifully allowed Mathilde to accompany her to her room where Mathilde dusted her face with powder and dressed her hair into a fall of ringlets, with loose tendrils of curls dangling bewitchingly before her ears. Mathilde then chose one of her nicest gowns . . . a diaphanous robe of blue gauze over a darker blue slip, which clung to every curve of her slender form and not worn for over a year . . . and carefully placed it over her head. The phrase, 'a lamb led to the slaughter', came to Amelia's mind and she wondered if her resolution would be strong enough should the need arise.

Clara was acting as if the anticipated proposal was for real and she excitedly slipped into Amelia's room, her face aglow.

'He has come!' she whispered. 'He looks so handsome, in spite of . . . well, you know!'

And when Amelia was summoned downstairs to appear in what had been her father's study, she had to agree with her sister's opinion.

Ned, standing a little apart from Louisa and Blake, was dressed in his military uniform of highly polished knee-length black boots, spotless white breeches that stretched over his muscular thighs, and his scarlet coat with its golden facings and epaulettes, neatly fastened with shining buttons. He carried his hat neatly tucked under his arm and only a tiny flutter high in his unscarred cheek betrayed any sign of nervousness.

Amelia's breath caught in her throat as she felt her heart race out of control and her hand fluttered uncertainly at her throat. An unexpected gleam of admiration shone in his eyes as she entered the room but it was swiftly brought under control and when he calmly faced her again, his expression was tight and stern.

Well-schooled by Louisa, Amelia bobbed a small curtsey. 'Don't overdo it,' Louisa had warned. 'I don't know what his army rank is but I doubt it is high enough to warrant a full curtsey!'

Ned bowed in stiff military style. He coughed slightly, to clear his throat and Amelia wanted to tell him not to worry; she wasn't going to entrap him as Louisa had bidden her, but she merely stood meekly before him.

'Miss Haverton, will you do me the honour of becoming my wife?' Ned said evenly.

Amelia hesitated. She knew she could

love this man, indeed she already felt strangely moved by his presence, his nearness, the very thought of becoming his life-partner. Her mouth felt dry and she doubted she could speak and was surprised to hear her own voice saying, 'I am honoured by your proposal, sir, but I am afraid I must decline your kind offer.'

She forced herself to meet his eyes as she spoke and she was sure she saw a flicker of relief pass over them. So, she was right. He hadn't wanted to marry her. And why should he? He had only met her the previous day and, as Louisa had taken pains to point out, she was no great catch.

'Amelia!' Louisa cried out in fury.

Amelia bravely smiled faintly as Ned took hold of her hand and drew it gently to his lips.

'Thank you,' he breathed, so quietly that none but Amelia heard him.

He bowed in Louisa and Blake's direction, turned smartly on his heels and left the room.

Amelia's heart went with him, but she was determined that none should know it.

Louisa's wrath was immediately made clear.

'You stupid, stupid girl!' she screeched. 'Do you know what you have done? You have thrown away probably the only offer you will ever have! Well, I wash my hands of you!'

Louisa was tight-lipped for the rest of the day, barely speaking a civil word to Amelia or Clara. Indeed she voiced her displeasure at Amelia's refusal of Ned's proposal at every opportunity.

Amelia bore it with outward calm, though inside, she was in turmoil. What was Ned thinking of her? Did he despise her?

At least he had seemed grateful to her for refusing to allow Louisa's scheme to succeed, she consoled herself ... if it was gratitude that she had seen flicker in his eyes. And how did that make her feel, that he was glad she had let him off the hook?

Did she rather wish that he had persisted with his proposal? That he had declared that he had fallen in love with her at first sight and was only too happy to make her his wife?

Maybe, deep down, she had longed for that to be so . . . but, so great was her shame, that she refused to admit it!

# 6

Ned drove to West Lodge with mixed feelings. It would have been disastrous if he had been forced to marry Miss Haverton, but he couldn't help wondering what life with her would be like. Not the humdrum sort of marriage he witnessed among some of his contemporaries, of that he was sure. He suspected she would be able to hold her own in any sort of serious discussion and would enliven his social life with her natural and unaffected manner.

However, at the moment, he didn't have a social life and that was the way he had to keep it for the foreseeable future. He had enough complications in his life to deal with . . . and he was returning home to the main one.

During the next few days, Amelia hoped that Mr Davenport would find some way to contact her, maybe by riding near their common boundary or even coming to oversee the removal of the steel trap that had so cruelly injured his dog and so she found her steps leading her in that direction whenever she was strolling in the garden . . . but, when she heard voices drifting through the shrubbery and tentatively made her way to investigate, she found only some of his grounds staff assisting Wallace, the local blacksmith, to dismantle it.

The men merely glanced her way and touched their forelocks to acknowledge her presence but swiftly resumed their task.

'How is Mr Davenport's dog?' she enquired of them.

'He's a-burning with fever, miss,' one replied, deferentially touching his forelock again before turning back to the task-in-hand.

'Oh, I'm sorry. If there's any-thing . . . ' But she let the sentence die unfinished. What could she do that these capable men who more used to working with animals could not do? 'Do feel free to search the woodland for any more traps. I have no idea who has set that one. It certainly wasn't on my late father's orders; nor on orders from Colonel Usherwood.'

'There's been talk of vagrants in the area, Miss Haverton,' Wallace informed her.

'Aye. I'd keep well away from this area at present, if I was you, miss, 'specially at night,' one of the others muttered without looking at her.

'Yes. My sister and I were startled by two men a number of days ago, but they didn't look the sort to set traps like that. They would be more likely to set rabbit snares or steal eggs from the farms.'

'Best to take no chances, miss.'

Amelia acknowledged the wisdom of that and she drifted back to the manor garden to where Clara was sketching in a secluded corner, feeling quite despondent at the thought that she might never see Mr Davenport again.

However, two days later, Clara said

she had seen Mr Davenport out riding in the company of a younger man.

'A stable lad?' Amelia wondered.

'Possibly, but I don't think so. He was better dressed than that. He seemed to indicate my presence to Mr Davenport. I was sitting on top of the stile, sketching the view across the meadow and trying to catch the wonderful colours of the leaves with my pastels and I hoped . . . well, I thought they might trot over to bid me good-day but Mr Davenport took hold of his bridle and turned him away. It would have been pleasant to talk with them,' she added wistfully.

'Hmm! No doubt Mr Davenport has learned not to risk his reputation by coming too close to either of us!' Amelia said, with some bitterness in her voice. 'And who can blame him!'

Later that day, a sudden change in Louisa's manner drove away any further thought of whom Mr Davenport's young visitor might be. When they entered the drawing room before dinner, Louisa was waving a hand-written note towards her husband.

'Isn't it exciting! Jesmond says he is coming to stay for a while. Now, you will be nice to him, dear, won't you? I haven't seen him for quite some months and he is usually so attentive to us.'

'Only when he is in the basket,' Blake pointed out. 'He'll be wanting to hang on to your sleeve, Louisa, and I won't have it!'

'Now, dearest! Don't be such a nip-farthing! He's no worse than you were when you were his age. You used to say that all young men have pockets to let! And he is family, remember!'

She turned to the girls as they entered the room. 'Amelia and Clara, you'll be pleased to hear that my brother, Jesmond, is coming to stay next week. He's always popular with the ladies! He might be persuaded to invite some of his friends to stay with us. You'll like that, won't you, girls? And don't pull your face like that, Amelia! It makes you look very unattractive. I've been very lenient with you after your folly in refusing Mr Davenport's offer. This could be your way of making amends. And you, too, Clara. This could well be a heaven sent opportunity for both of you!'

As soon as breakfast was over the following day, Louisa summoned Mrs Tranter to the drawing room to inform her of the impending visits and the extra entertaining she was planning.

'Mr Marsden is very particular about his meals, Cook, so I hope you take every care not to let me down!'

'I hope, as I always do my best, ma'am.'

'Yes, of course. Now, we'll have a lot to do to get the house ready for my brother's arrival. Amelia, I want you to oversee the work. You must get the maids to move Clara's things into the room at the end of the corridor.'

'The little box-room, Louisa. Surely not! It's tiny!'

'Are you questioning my judgment?'

'No, Louisa, but there are other rooms.'

'They will be needed for his valet and other guests who may wish to visit whilst he is here. He is my brother, after all and must be treated with due deference. In many households, Clara wouldn't be out of the schoolroom yet. Please see that it is done promptly.'

Amelia wondered if Jesmond had been present at her father's funeral but, a few days later, the moment Jesmond jumped down from his sporting curricle, she knew he hadn't.

The words 'popinjay' or 'peacock' flew into her mind and she exchanged a wry glance with Clara. Although it was mid-afternoon and most of his peers would have dressed in a coat suitable for driving, Jesmond's coat was of shining gold nankeen with a waistcoat of black silk covered with intertwining red and blue flowers. The points of his shirt collar were so high that Amelia hoped he had not had the need to glance over his shoulder as he drove along the road for she was sure he would have stabbed himself in the eye had he but tried it!

When he sprang from his driving seat, it was to reveal voluminous trousers such as she had never seen and the tails of his coat were so long they almost trailed along the ground. He paused dramatically and raised his quizzing glass to his right eye.

'La! How grand I find you, sister, dear! And my new cousins! Two hothouse flowers, exquisite enough to grace the Regent's summer palace!' He swept his high-crowned beaver off his head and made an elaborate gesture over his extended leg. 'A pity I have but two arms,' he cried as he minced finely up the steps and tossed his hat into Ellis's hands. ' . . . but, since I must choose, I must offer my arms to my sister and the elder Miss Haverton, knowing that such a delicate flower as my younger cousin must have so many admirers that she will not pine to be left unaccompanied!'

With a despairing glance at Clara, Amelia hesitantly laid her hand on Jesmond's arm and allowed him to lead her and Louisa into the drawing room.

'How quaint!' he declared roving his glance around the room. 'Louisa, my dear, you are becoming quite countrified! No matter! It's very convivial and I'm sure your London 'set' won't despise you for it. In fact, it may set a new fashion! I'm hoping to set a new fashion myself!'

He released Louisa's and Amelia's arms and obligingly twirled around to give everyone the full benefit of his remarkable attire. 'Since the Beau quarrelled with Prinny last year, every man who fancies himself to be bang up to the knocker is vying to take his place. What d'you think, Miss Haverton? No! Amelia! I may call you by your given names, mightn't I? For I am your cousin-by-marriage!'

He beamed at them for approval and when both Amelia and Clara agreed that he might, he continued, 'I'll wager you'll see no-one so attired out here in the sticks!'

Amelia forcibly suppressed the bubble of laughter that threatened to erupt from her throat and she coughed into her hand.

'No, Mr Marsden. You have me there! I haven't seen anyone dressed remotely like you, either here or on my rare visits to town.'

'Jesmond, Amelia! Call me Jesmond! It will sound divine upon such sweet lips! Ah, but about my attire! I thought as much! It'll be all the crack next season!' he predicted. 'You'll see!'

Shaking to contain her amusement, Amelia joined Clara on a two-seater sofa, from which neither of them could refrain from ogling their visitor. His face was powdered and his cheeks unnaturally reddened with rouge. Amelia was also sure he wore lipstick on his rather loose lips and once her eyes had fastened on to a shiny black patch displayed high on his left cheek she felt unable to tear her gaze away. Surely the patch was sliding down his face!

A choked hiccup from Clara confirmed her suspicion and she clutched at Clara's hand in a vain effort to still her choked laughter.

'Ah, I see you young ladies are fascinated by the fall of my neck-cloth!' Jesmond twittered. 'Took all of two hours to fix it this morning! Reason I was late, you know! Never can tie the devilish things first time! Must have ruined a dozen at least.'

'Surely you set your valet to tie your neck-cloth!' Louisa exclaimed. 'I know Blake never attempts to tie his own and he is so particular that he never lets me do it.'

'Had to let Craddock go, me dear! Haven't a sixpence to scratch with right now! Dashed bad luck at the races, you know! A fine set of bone-setters! Shouldn't be allowed, but there it is! All in a day's fun!'

Amelia took all this to mean that he was out of funds, having gambled it away on unsuccessful horses. The look on Louisa's face confirmed her suspicion and she wasn't surprised when Louisa told her to go to the kitchen to see why Cook hadn't yet sent up Kate with a trolley by way of diversion.

When she returned, closely followed by Kate, Vernon had joined the group and Jesmond was demonstrating his dexterity in flipping open the lid of his snuff box, an elaborately ornate box in the shape of a sedan chair.

'Only take my own sort,' he confided. 'Doesn't do to get a name for never handing it out. Gave some to Prinny a couple of months ago! Said it was rare stuff!'

'You've spoken to the Prince Regent?' Clara asked with some awe in her voice.

'Spoken to him? We're like that!' Jesmond indicated, crossing over the first two fingers of his right hand. 'Course, he's been down at Brighton for some weeks now so it's been a bit flat in town. No-one of any note there!'

'Isn't everyone due back round about now?' Amelia enquired, not so immersed in country ways that she hadn't heard of the Little Season when most of the fashionable society returned to the city until the hunting season began in late autumn.

'Quite so!' Jesmond airily replied, twirling a hand in the air. 'Far too crowded!'

Louisa's mouth pursed and she diverted attention by demanding that Vernon returned the snuff box before he spilled it.

Too late! The delicately perfumed snuff was scattered on the carpet.

By the time the adults were seated at the dinner table, Amelia was wondering if Jesmond ever had anything sensible to say but doubted it very much. They were in for a tedious time.

Louisa made it very clear to Amelia that she expected her to help in entertaining her brother. 'But don't go setting your cap at him! He needs someone far richer than you to pull him out of the mire of debt!'

'There is no danger of that!' Amelia retorted, refraining from telling Louisa what she really thought about her brother. However, she agreed to accompany Jesmond on a drive around the locality the following afternoon.

So, leaving Clara to go sketching, Amelia allowed Jesmond to hand her up into his curricle and, with Sam standing behind, Jesmond tooled his vehicle out of the manor-house grounds.

Jesmond was more concerned with impressing Amelia with his driving skills than making conversation and, when he did speak, she quickly learned that he merely required an affirmative admiring comment. Consequently, she was able to quietly drink in the natural beauty of the countryside, shutting out the few meaningless asides that assailed her ears. On the returning journey, they came up behind a farm vehicle laden with a late cut of hay.

'We'll soon show him a rear set of wheels!' Jesmond boasted, flicking his whip across his horse's back. Until then, his level of expertise in handling his horse had been competent but unremarkable. Now, with the prospect of showing himself to be a notable whip, Jesmond filled with excitement. Leaning forward until he was almost standing, he urged his horse faster and faster as he pulled over to the right-hand side of the country lane.

'Careful, Jesmond!' Amelia warned. 'There's quite a blind corner up ahead.'

'Nonsense, Amelia! I know what I'm doing!'

Amelia was already holding on to the side of the seat as tightly as she could, her mouth quite dry with fear. She was no greenhorn when it came to driving, having been taught by her brother and well-used to the locality in which she lived . . . but, this, she knew was sheer folly.

'I beg of you, Jesmond! Don't try it! Arghh!'

The near-side wheel of the curricle grazed the rear off-side wheel-hub of the hay-cart.

'Take care, man!' Sam grunted from his position at the rear.

Jesmond's cheeks flushed with an angry bloom and he flicked his whip across his horse's head. For a few interminable seconds the two vehicles lurched along together and, for a hopeful moment, Amelia thought they might get away with the act of folly. But, it wasn't to be. The driver of the more solid and lumbering hay-cart held the curve of its line, though its high-piled load swayed from side to side as the cart lurched round the bend, but the lighter curricle, being driven at such reckless speed, would have needed the expert hands of a far more accomplished driver than Jesmond Marsden were it to have safely negotiated the sharp bend.

Jesmond lost his head. He pulled sharply on the reins, forcing the horse's head to rise. It was too sudden a move and the horse half-reared. Jesmond froze and let the reins run loosely through his hands. Free of its restraint, the horse dropped its hooves back on to the roadway and tried to resume its headlong gallop, but the pause had upset the momentum of the vehicle and it began to swing from side to side, the off-side wheel now on the soft grassy verge.

As the curricle tilted sideways, its off-side wheel now drunkenly trying to turn on the verge, Jesmond recovered his poise long enough to leap from the vehicle on to the verge. With an empty space at her right-hand side, gravity took over and Amelia began to slide sideways.

Everything seemed to happen in slow motion, though, in reality, it was over in a couple of seconds. She was aware that Sam had reached over the back of the curricle in an attempt to hold on to her but the curricle was tilting at such an angle that he was in as much danger as she was.

She saw the grass looming up towards her and she instinctively curled her head in towards her chest as she fell from the toppling curricle and landed heavily on to the ground.

# 7

'You dolt! You empty-headed buffoon! What on earth possessed you, man, to attempt to overtake on that corner? Have you got a deathwish?'

The male voice penetrated Amelia's semi-conscious mind. It was vaguely familiar and, although the tone was angry, she felt reassured by it. Someone was there to help. She tried to sit up but her head swam alarmingly and she fell back with a low moan. At once, someone was kneeling at her side and she felt firm hands running over her body.

'Hey! What d'you think you're doing? Have you no sense of decency?' Jesmond's voice objected.

'More than you, apparently! I saw you leap from the driving seat to save your own skin!' the voice said calmly. 'It's all right, Miss Haverton. There doesn't seem to be any bones broken. Open your eyes and look at me.'

Amelia did so, knowing whose face she would see . . . the face she had held in her memory over the past few days, wondering if she would ever see him again. She moaned softly as the face swam in and out of focus.

'Ned!' she whispered through dry lips. She could taste grass and the gritty texture of earth in her mouth. 'I fell off!' she added unnecessarily.

'Yes. I saw you . . . and this crazy dolt of a driver intent on killing you both!'

'What? Hey, I object to your choice of words, my good man!' Jesmond said indignantly. 'Let me put you right on both scores.'

'No! I'll put you right,' Ned returned. 'Firstly, I am not your 'good man', nor anybody else's and, secondly, I have never seen such an appalling mishandling of a vehicle! Now, why don't you see to your horse and groom who are over there, whilst I attend to Miss Haverton?'

'Now, look here!' Jesmond protested, but Ned had already turned his back on him and Jesmond was left soundlessly opening and closing his mouth.

Amelia struggled to sit up, grateful for Ned's supporting arm around her shoulders, vaguely aware of what a fright she must present!

'Don't move!' Ned bade her when she was seated comfortably and left her side momentarily. When he returned he had a small flask in his hand and, in his other, a silk kerchief. The unmistakeable fumes of brandy wafted across Amelia's nostrils and she hoped he didn't expect her drink any of it.

Ned tilted up her chin with the hand that held the flask.

'This may sting a little,' he warned, 'but I want to see just how badly you are hurt, and the sooner the dirt is cleaned away, the sooner your skin will heal.' As he spoke, he gently dabbed his moistened kerchief around her face.

Amelia kept her eyes fixed on Ned's face, drawing comfort and courage from the tender concern in his expression.

'There! Not as bad as I feared. Your face is badly grazed though, and I think you will have quite a shiner there by tomorrow! However, it could have been much worse!'

He smiled at her. Amelia felt a strange sensation surge through her body and her head seemed to swim off her shoulders.

She looked about her. To her right, she could see Sam seated on the ground, looking as dazed as she felt but otherwise unharmed. Jesmond was towering over him, pointing towards the drunken-looking curricle and the horse that stood trembling between its shafts.

'I tell you, get my curricle back on the road!' Jesmond was ordering Sam.

Amelia smiled faintly as Sam looked up at him with a baleful eye.

'That curricle ain't going nowhere, mister,' he muttered, as he struggled to his feet. 'A blind man with one eye could tell you th'axle's broke!'

'Do you feel able to get to your feet, Miss Haverton?' Ned asked, drawing her attention back to him.

'I think so, though I fear I shall do so quite inelegantly! If you will give me your arm?'

Ned did more than that. He took hold of her hands and drew her to her feet with no seeming effort on his part and very little on Amelia's, as he said; 'I hope you will allow me to drive you home, Miss Haverton. It will take but a moment to turn around my curricle. Maybe your groomsman will oblige?'

'As long as it isn't too much of an imposition,' Amelia agreed, nodding to Sam to do his bidding. 'But what about my cousin? How will he return home?'

Ned felt a huge sensation of relief flow through him at the mention of the relationship between Miss Haverton and her companion. Nevertheless, cousins were sometimes known to marry.

'Do you much care?' he asked, raising any eyebrow.

Amelia threw an amused look towards

Jesmond, who was watching Sam as he led Ned's matching roans in a tight circle. 'Not really. He had scant regard for either me or Sam, though I am sure he will expect to be offered a seat in your circle.'

Ned grinned. 'It holds only two and one behind. Shall I offer him the position of groomsman?'

Amelia laughed aloud at the thought. 'Don't risk it!' she warned. 'He might accept!'

At the sound of her laughter, Jesmond began to mince towards them. 'I say, my good man . . . er, that is, whoever you are,' he corrected himself, adding a belated, 'sir. I have need of your vehicle to return Miss Haverton to her home.' He laughed self-consciously. 'Got to take care of the fairer sex, you know!'

'More's the pity you didn't think of that before your foolhardy attempt to overtake the hay cart on a blind bend!' Ned retorted unceremoniously. 'And, in answer to your question, no, you may not borrow my curricle. I wouldn't trust any blood-cattle of mine into your care after witnessing your lack of ability as a driver!'

'Hey, I say! That's too dashed impolite of you! You are surely not suggesting that Miss Haverton walks home!'

'Not at all. I will take her myself, with your groom riding the footboard — if he feels up to it.'

Sam nodded his agreement and Ned began to lead Amelia towards his curricle as he spoke.

'But, I say! What about me?' Jesmond protested.

'Stay with your horse and vehicle! I will send someone to attend you as soon as I have delivered Miss Haverton to her home.'

Amelia accepted Ned's hand as he assisted her into his curricle, feeling no alarm as he took his place beside her and, as soon as Sam took up his position on the footboard, Ned gently shook the reins to command his roans to proceed.

She knew that he glanced down at her every so often but neither of them spoke for a while. Amelia longed to say something to express her gratitude for his timely appearance and to dispel the residue of embarrassment she felt from their previous meeting.

As it happened, both of them spoke together.

'I must thank you . . . '

'I must thank you . . . '

They both laughed.

'I'm sorry. You first!'

'I'm sorry. You first!'

They laughed again . . . then Ned took command of the conversation. 'As the gentlemen, allow me to be the one to offer you my heartfelt gratitude for your understanding of my dilemma the other day. I meant you no disrespect but I could tell that you had sensed my relief when you refused my offer of marriage.'

Amelia felt her cheeks warm and she knew Ned's sideways glance had detected her blush.

'I knew that Louisa had acted shamefully and left you with no option but to offer for me. It would have been dishonourable of me to take advantage of the situation.'

Oh, dear, did that sound pompous? She ventured a swift glance at his profile but avoided his gaze as he turned towards her.

'And dishonourable of me not to make the offer.'

This time, Amelia turned and met his gaze. She suddenly saw the amusing side of the episode. 'So, you only offered for me, knowing that I would refuse!' she said in mock indignation, the twinkle in her eyes contradicting her words. 'You took a risk, did you not? What if I had accepted your offer?'

His lips twitched with humour.

'Then we would now be engaged and you would be riding by my side in my carriage ... without the need of a groom! And I would be free to call you Amelia instead of Miss Haverton. But, you had already indicated your distaste for the match and I sensed you to be a lady of honour, as was proved by your rejection of my suit.'

Amelia remained silent. How she wished she could say that her aversion was only to the contrived situation and not to him personally. Their eyes met again and a sense of longing shivered down her spine and overflowed into the core of her being.

Ned concentrated on the road for a few moments and then turned towards her again.

'If my situation were different, Miss Haverton, I would be honoured to pay you court,' he said quietly.

'And I would be honoured to receive you, but, may we perhaps be friends?' she asked boldly.

Ned felt his heart turn somersaults. There was nothing he would like better that to be a friend of this delightful young woman, more than a friend, if the truth be told! He knew for certain than he could trust her with his life! However, his was not the only life that might be endangered. What could he say?

'As I said, if my situation were different . . .'

But Amelia's boldness had disintegrated when his response was not immediate.

'It is no matter,' she said with forced brightness. 'I expect we shall meet but rarely since we live such a quiet life here.' Her voice faltered and she was relieved to see the gateway to Moreton Manor not far ahead. 'Ah, and here we are! Home at last,' she trilled with false gaiety, as Ned expertly guided the curricle between the gateposts. 'I must thank you, sir, for your kind services.'

Amelia stared straight ahead as Ned jumped down and came around to her side of the curricle. She prepared to hold out her hand for his assistance but he took her by surprise when he reached out with both hands and took hold of her around her waist and bodily swung her to the ground.

'Miss Haverton, I have upset you.'

The denial that was on her lips was swept away by a cry from behind her.

'Amelia! What is the meaning of this?'

Amelia swung round to see Louisa descending the steps in great haste, her expression of outrage turning to horror as she took in Amelia's dishevelled and bruised appearance. 'Ahh! What has happened? Mr Davenport, what have you done to my cousin?'

'Ask rather, 'what has Jesmond done to me'!' Amelia retorted through swollen lips, slipping out of Ned's hold and flouncing towards Louisa.

'Jesmond?' Louisa clasped her hand to her throat. 'Where is he? Has there been an accident? Is he hurt? Where have you left him? Surely, he's not . . . not dead?'

'No, ma'am,' Ned gravely assured her. 'He is totally unharmed.'

'Then where is he? Why is he not with you? Why did he not bring Miss Haverton home instead of you? Are you intent on shaming us, sir?'

'Louisa, Mr Davenport has not shamed us. Indeed, he rescued me from a situation totally brought about by Jesmond's reckless driving! He overturned our curricle and . . . '

'I knew it! He's badly hurt! Take me to him at once! Oooh, I feel quite faint! My smelling salts, Amelia! Fetch them quickly!'

Amelia made as if to rush indoors to bring the required salts but Ned reached out and took hold of her arm to restrain her. When she glanced up at him, she saw his features had tightened.

Ned's voice was stiff with politeness when he spoke to Louisa. 'Your brother is unharmed, ma'am! He is attending to his horse and awaiting assistance. Your concern would be better directed towards Miss Haverton. I have administered such aid as I was able, but I am sure that further attention would be appreciated.'

Louisa seemed taken aback to be spoken to so coldly. 'Why, y . . . yes. I'm sure Clare will assist you, Amelia, and, as for you, sir . . . ' She drew herself up to her maximum height. 'I will detain you no longer! I take it that you will arrange to speed assistance on its way to my brother! You have the men, have you not?'

'I have, ma'am.'

'Then, that's the very least you can do!'

'The accident was none of Mr Davenport's doing!' Amelia felt obliged to point out, although it hurt her to speak

'Nonsense! Jesmond is an excellent driver! He is on the brink of applying for membership to the 'Four-Horse' Club!'

Amelia glanced apologetically towards Ned, shrugging her shoulders helplessly, her expression portraying abject misery at Louisa's attitude towards her rescuer. Ned bowed gallantly before her and lifted her hand to his lips.

'I will take my leave of you, Miss Haverton, but may I have your permission to call on you in a few days time to assure myself that you are well?'

'W . . . why, yes,' Amelia stammered, meeting Ned's eyes in bewilderment.

Ned smiled somewhat grimly, though his eyes softened at the corners. He nodded curtly to Louisa and then leaped back into his curricle, nodding his acknowledgement to Sam for standing with his horses. With a flick of his whip, he was gone.

# 8

Amelia found that the delayed shock caused by her untimely spill suddenly made her legs begin to tremble and she was thankful when Kate appeared to help her to undress and get into her bed. Kate plumped up her pillows and made her as comfortable as possible. Aches and pains were beginning to make their presence felt and she had begun to realise that she had been very fortunate not to have suffered serious injury.

Not long afterwards, Clara bounded into her room, eager about her mishap.

'What happened?' Clara asked breathlessly, once she was over the shock of seeing her sister's bruised face. 'Louisa said Mr Davenport was responsible. What did he do?'

'Mr Davenport had nothing to do with it,' Amelia mouthed painfully. 'He came upon us after the accident had happened. But for him, I would probably still be lying by the roadside. It was our 'dear' cousin, Jesmond, trying to impress me with his skill at driving!'

She went on to describe what had happened and was at least able to fashion a semblance of a smile when she told of Jesmond's futile request to borrow Ned's curricle. 'He was most put out! Serves him right!'

'I wondered where Mr Davenport was,' Clara mused.

'What d'you mean?' Amelia frowned.

Clara looked slightly sheepish and, when she replied, it was defensively. 'I decided to sketch by the spinney again, you know, from my favourite view from the stile.'

'Oh, yes?'

'I didn't expect to see Philip, of course.'

'Philip? Philip who?'

'I didn't ask his surname. He's the young man who was out riding with Mr

Davenport the other day. He was out walking and . . .'

' . . . you waved to him and he came over to speak to you?'

'Well, yes. How did you know? I wasn't too forward and he seemed very pleased to see me.'

The humorous twist of Amelia's mouth hurt. 'I'm sure he was! But, go on. What did he say about himself?'

'Well, that's the strange thing. It seems he can neither hear nor speak.'

'So how do you know his name?'

Clara had the grace to blush. 'He wrote it . . . on my hand.' The sparkle in her eyes betrayed the remembered tingle his touch had caused. 'I think he can read lip movements a little too,' she hurriedly added, hoping to deflect her sister's attention, 'because, when I said, 'Philip', he nodded and smiled.'

'And what else did he write on your hand?'

'Not a lot. We used signs mostly. It was great fun! The only thing is . . . I got the impression that he is a little afraid of Mr Davenport. When I indicated that we would visit them he was quite agitated; shook his head and put his finger to his lips. He waved both hands as if fending people off, like this.' She imitated his action. 'I think he meant we were not to mention our meeting to Mr Davenport at all.'

The next few days passed quickly indeed. Amelia felt frustrated by her weakness, but felt compelled by her bodily symptoms to spend most of the day reclining on the sofa or, when Jesmond's prattlings became too much to bear, resting on her bed.

Clara, much to her delight, was left very much to her own devices, as Vernon, once released from the toils of the schoolroom by his tutor, was happy to hang on to Jesmond's coat-tails and Amelia feared he was well on the way to becoming a replica of his uncle.

From Clara's flushed and excited expression on her returns home, Amelia knew she had been meeting Philip.

'I am teaching him to draw,' Clara

confided with a giggle on one occasion. 'He draws funny characters and makes me laugh. See, here is one of Mr Davenport.'

She drew out a folded paper, which she carefully unfolded and smoothed out. Amelia frowned as she regarded it. The drawing emphasised the scar on Ned's right cheek and exaggerated the arch of his dark eyebrows, making him seem quite villainous.

Amelia was horrified by her appearance the first time she saw her reflection in the looking glass and was thankful that Mr Davenport hadn't paid his promised visit.

As each day passed, Jesmond's account of the incident changed more and more, until he was fully convinced that he had taken complete charge of the recovery and Ned was the careless villain. Amelia grew weary of protesting about his ludicrous claims and was thankful when she overheard Blake forbidding him when Jesmond announced that he was sending the bill for the repair of his curricle to Ned Davenport.

It was a conversation she should not have been listening to, having retired to her room earlier in the evening. However, the need of a glass of water had persuaded her to drape a shawl around her shoulders and to descend barefooted down the main staircase. The raised voices from the library brought her footsteps to a halt.

'Don't be a fool, Jesmond!' Blake said in exasperation. 'You may have convinced Louisa that Ned Davenport was the one at fault but the groom's tale is somewhat different.'

'And you take the word of a servant over mine?'

'I do when the circumstances back up their word!'

Amelia thought Jesmond had been silenced, but it was only a momentary lull. When his response came, his tone of voice was entirely different.

'The fact is, old boy, I'm on the rocks! Extremely short of the blunt! In fact, to tell you the truth, old boy, I haven't a feather to fly with!'

'So, why am I not surprised?' Blake drawled sarcastically. 'And what do you expect me to do about it, pray? Pay off your debts? Set you up with an income, perhaps?'

'By Jove! That would be extremely generous of you, Blake! I knew you'd see me all right!'

'Then your confidence is misplaced, for I have no intention of paying off your debts!'

'B . . . but you said . . . '

'No! I've done it once and that's enough!'

Amelia was about to continue on her way to the kitchen, aware that it wasn't her concern how Jesmond was to sort out his financial affairs but Blake's next words halted her.

'Louisa has told you what to do! Get yourself a rich wife! There's one here under the very roof! Hasn't got a huge fortune, to be sure. Only three thousand a year, but it would be enough to get you out of dun territory! So, stop fooling around and work your questionable charms on her!'

Amelia was filled with indignation. How dare he make such an outrageous suggestion? She was about to storm into the library and rage at them when Jesmond replied.

'And be leg-shackled for life? Too high a price, old boy! Besides, not my type! Too much of a chawbacon for me! I'm no Johnny raw, you know!'

Amelia gasped at his effrontery and was even more enraged at Blake's response.

'No, I'd call you too much of a loose fish, if the truth be told, but the choice is yours! The girl's probably desperate enough to accept you, since Louisa has choked off the only opposition! In fact, as an added incentive to get her parcelled off, I'll slip you a couple of thousand on the quiet!'

'Only a couple of thousand, old boy?' Jesmond laughed scathingly, his voice now holding menace. 'I heard along the grapevine that you had worked your way into a fortune, but I'll keep my lips sealed if you make it worth my while!'

'Don't be ridiculous, man! I don't know what you are talking about! And, in any case, no-one would believe any Banbury Tales of yours!'

'No Banbury Tales, old boy! I have contacts at Westminster. Does the name Rupert Bradshaw mean anything to you? No? You need to watch your back, old boy. There's a few there who only need me to nod the wink at them and they'll drop you in it faster than you can jump aside.'

'Are you threatening me, Jesmond?' Blake's voice was suddenly cold.

'Just passing comment, old boy! No need to get huffy. I'll leave you to think about it. I'm sure you'll find it to your advantage to keep me sweet.'

Amelia could tell that Jesmond was approaching the door and she hastily dropped the idea of a glass of water and swiftly sped back along the hall and up the first flight of stairs.

Jesmond's part in the conversation

didn't surprise her too greatly, but Blake had shown a completely different side to his character from that which he invariably showed. She was incensed by his offer to pay Jesmond to take her off his hands! Well, forewarned was indeed forearmed!

It was as her eyes finally closed in sleep that she remembered Jesmond's allusions to some underhand dealing concerning Blake and his position at Westminster. What had her cousin been up to? Was he privy to confidential reports? Was he blackmailing someone? Until tonight, she would have discounted the idea as a bag of moonshine, but now, she wasn't so sure and, in spite of his protestation, she suspected that there might be some foundation to Jesmond's claim.

Her head felt far from clear the next day and she succumbed to Mrs Tranter's decision that she should break her fast quietly in her room.

'You aren't ill, are you, Melie?' Clara asked anxiously. 'I will stay with you this morning, if you wish; only I had thought to go . . . sketching, you know.'

'I think, Clara, that I had better come with you this morning and meet this young man myself,' Amelia decided. 'For although he professes to be in some fear of Mr Davenport, he must realise that he is putting you in a compromising position by meeting with you in this way.'

Besides wanting to curtail any indiscretions her younger sister might commit, Amelia also needed the distraction of getting out of the house to give herself time to decide just how she would tackle Jesmond if he decided to take Blake's advice to woo her with his charms. Ugh! How could either of them imagine that she would be willing to degrade herself so piteously?

And what was that about Louisa having 'choked off the opposition'? Had Ned indeed made his promised visit and been turned away?

'So, you must wait whilst I put on my walking dress, Clara, dear . . . and don't look so rebellious. I will be very kind and affable towards Philip, only I must insist that he complies with my wishes.'

She chose her best walking dress of figured jaconet, which had double flounces and long sleeves, since the day was typically chilly for the time of year. It suited her colouring and she harboured a hope that Ned Davenport might somehow be in the vicinity.

Clara was a little subdued as they set off together but her cheerful disposition soon shone through and she was in fine spirit as they approached the stile in the hedge that bordered both properties. Philip was there before them, perched comfortably atop the stile. His smile of welcome transformed into a look of guilt as he took in Amelia's presence at Clara's side. However, he leaped down and bowed most elegantly before wordlessly beseeching Clara for an introduction.

It was impossible to say whether or not he fully understood that Amelia was Clara's sister but he smiled and bowed again when Clara spelled out her name on the palm of his hand. Amelia then told Clara that she must get him to understand that he must inform Ned of their friendship.

Clara signed and mimed the request by pointing firstly to Amelia, then touching her lips and blowing over her finger and pointing in the direction of General Usherwood's hall and then drawing the shame of a scar down her right cheek. That Philip understood was clear, firstly by his raised eyebrow, followed by a frown and shake of his head.

Clara seized his arm and nodded vigorously, knowing that Amelia would not settle for anything less.

When Philip looked at her doubtfully, Amelia joined in the charade. She touched herself and Clara and indicated them walking away together. Philip sighed and shrugged his shoulders in defeat. Then he gravely nodded his head. He indicated that Amelia and Clara return to their home and that he would ask Ned to ride round to see them.

Amelia grasped hold of his arm and shook her head, remembering that Louisa had already refused Ned entry on at least one occasion.

'Tell him to come here,' she mimed.

Philip nodded and held up three fingers, by which Amelia supposed him to mean in three hours. He then bowed to them both and climbed back on to the stile. With an impudent grin, he blew a kiss in Clara's direction, jumped down from the stile and set off across the meadow that skirted the coppice.

Amelia looked sternly at Clara.

'I hope that last 'mime' doesn't mean that you have allowed him to take the liberty of kissing you!'

Clara blushed and cast down her eyes. 'Only on my hand, and once lightly on my cheek,' she admitted, 'but I do like him so and I know he will do me no harm.'

'I hope you are right — but now we must await to see what Mr Davenport says about it. If he will not change his mind and allow you to visit at his home under my chaperonage, that will have to be the end of the matter.'

They returned to their home and occupied themselves in the rose garden, Amelia snipping some stems of late roses, whilst Clara sketched one of the stable cats stretched out in the noontime sun.

The sound of Mrs Tranter's gong drew them in for luncheon, though neither of them felt able to eat much. Amelia was nervous about meeting Ned again. She had already decided that she would speak to Ned alone and she had earlier made her decision known to Clara.

The unaccustomed presence of Jesmond at the luncheon table made her doubly anxious. He didn't usually rise until after luncheon was over and she hoped his presence there didn't mean that he was about to put Blake's suggestion into action, though she suspected from Louisa's frivolous garrulity that her fear was correct.

'Don't leave my side!' she hissed at Clara, as they left the dining room together. 'I fear Jesmond is about to make a declaration!'

'No! Not really!' Clara grinned, impervious to the glare in Amelia's eyes. 'Shall you accept or give him a put-down?'

'Neither, for now! There isn't time. I have to see Mr Davenport . . . to further your cause, remember! Help me to keep him at bay!'

With Clara at her side, Amelia proceeded to inspect the bedroom linen cupboard; inspect the contents of the cold larder and the dry store; and hold an elongated discussion with Mrs Tranter concerning the menus for the rest of the week. When she judged it was time to meet Ned at the stile by the spinney, she slipped away through the kitchen door and hurried through the kitchen garden.

She glanced over her shoulder as she reached the arch in the privet hedge that separated the kitchen garden from the rose garden. No-one was behind her. She slipped through the arch . . . and ran straight into Jesmond!

'Ah, Amelia! How propitious! I thought you might return here! You forgot these!'

He waved the scissors in his hand and Amelia remembered laying them on the sundial when they had heard the luncheon gong.

'Oh! Yes! Thank you, Jesmond. I . . . er . . . hoped to find them here.'

She held out her hand for the scissors, but Jesmond playfully held them out of reach.

'I demand a forfeit! It's only fair!'

He smiled in what he obviously thought to be a teasing way, but Amelia wasn't in a playful mood.

'I have no time for games, Jesmond!' she said sharply. 'Either give me the scissors or take them back yourself! It means nought to me!'

'Aha! A show of fire, eh! I like a chit with fire! Come, m'dear. Be sweet to me!'

'But I'm no chit, sir! More like a 'chawbacon', am I not?'

He frowned, but clearly didn't remember using the phrase about her the previous night.

'Ha-ha! I should say not! More like a spirited hussy!'

'Indeed I am not! Oh!'

As she spoke, he clutched hold of her wrist and pulled her close. His move was so unexpected that Amelia found herself encircled in his arms before she had time to attempt to evade him.

'Let me go at once!' she said indignantly.

'Not until I've had a kiss.'

He held her head tightly in his grip and although she twisted and turned as much as she was able, his damp lips trawled across her cheeks as he searched for her mouth.

'Let me go!' she screamed, thoroughly alarmed now. How far was he prepared to go?

'You heard the lady!' another voice intervened.

# 9

'Ned.' Amelia struggled to free herself, as Jesmond said haughtily, 'You are intruding in a private conversation, sir, and I must ask you to leave immediately!'

'I heard Miss Haverton cry for help,' Ned calmly replied, turning his gaze to Amelia. 'Do you require my assistance, Miss Haverton?'

'Yes, I do!'

'Nonsense! Miss Haverton merely tripped and I grasped hold of her to save her from falling!'

'No, you didn't!' Amelia snapped. 'You forced your attentions upon me and I demand that you let me go!'

'You heard the lady! Release her at once!' Ned commanded, striding nearer.

'And if I don't?' Jesmond said recklessly, pulling Amelia back towards him, holding her as a shield in front of him as he backed away. 'Ouch!'

He doubled over, winded by Amelia's elbow that she had jabbed back at his mid-riff.

As she felt his grip loosen, Amelia jerked herself free and swiftly stepped aside as Ned lunged forwards, smashing his fist into Jesmond's chin, sending him reeling backwards. Jesmond lost his footing and fell to the ground, where he scrabbled sideways to avoid further attack.

'You, you insult me, sir!' he stammered. 'You, you'll pay for this! I will see you prosecuted for trespassing! I'll, I'll call you out!'

'You do so,' Ned agreed. 'I will await your seconds.'

'Oh!' Amelia cried in alarm, as she rushed into Ned's arms. 'You mustn't! He'll cheat! He might kill you!'

Ned laughed harshly. 'I doubt it! Men of his sort don't fight duels.'

Jesmond was already struggling to his feet and backing away. 'I'll see you pay for this!' he threatened again before leaving.

Ned could feel Amelia's body trembling against him and his heart beat erratically within him. He gently raised his right hand, using this thumb to wipe away a tear that was trickling down her cheek. His other hand tenderly cupped her chin. 'Don't worry about him. I am only too glad that I ventured this way when you didn't keep our rendezvous as arranged.'

'So am I!' Amelia agreed. She felt so safe held within Ned's arms. She wished she were able to lay her head against his chest and lean against the strength of him but she valued her independent spirit too much to feign more weakness than she truly felt and so she drew back a little and spoke candidly.

'I was on my way to meet you and I sensed Jesmond was planning to waylay me. I had gone to great pains to avoid him, but to no avail.' She shuddered. 'He frightened me so!' Embarrassed at revealing her inner turmoil, she added, 'Of course, he's feeling pretty desperate. He's rather purse-pinched, you know. I accidentally overheard a conversation between him and my cousin, Blake, last night ... but I didn't suspect he would go so far as this!'

'Is he here for long?' Ned asked, glancing in the direction Jesmond had taken. 'I feel I must advise you to avoid solitary areas like this, and not only on his account. Since Russ was hurt, my men have patrolled our boundaries daily and they suspect that a person, or persons, have been loitering in the area.'

He paused, knowing he had to say more, though he wished with all his heart that he didn't. 'And, for this reason, I must forbid any further contact between your sister and my ward. I have already forbidden Philip to return to their trysting place.'

Amelia felt as though he were censoring her for allowing Clara the freedom she had had over the past few days and she hastened to agree with him. 'Yes, I, too, have forbidden Clara to come here alone.' But a pang of conscience towards her promise to Clara drove her on to say, 'But I wondered if it might be possible for Clara and I to visit Philip in your home? There are so few young people in the village and we would be very . . . ' She had been going to say, 'discrete' but her word froze on her lips when Ned interrupted brusquely.

'I'm sorry, but that is quite impossible at the moment. As you know, I have no plans to socialise whilst I am here. My household is quite unsuitable and I have no wish to risk tarnishing the reputation of either you or your sister.' Amelia felt his withdrawal as a tangible thing. She had felt so easy with him but now his expression was stern and almost forbidding.

'Oh!' The involuntary cry escaped her lips as she felt his rejection of her anew. She stepped back, knowing her cheeks were aflame with embarrassment. 'Then, I must bid you good day, sir.'

Ned reached out to restrain her, but

he knew he must stay with his resolve and so he changed the movement into crooking his arm.

'Allow me to escort you to within sight of your home.'

Amelia would have liked to refuse but knew it would have been childish of her and unwise in the light of the past half-hour, so she laid her hand upon his arm and, with her face averted, silently walked by his side as they skirted the kitchen garden until they were at the edge of the rear lawn.

Here they paused. Amelia removed her hand from his arm, instantly missing the strength of her touch upon him had given her. Ned bowed stiffly and they silently took their leave of each other. Amelia held her head erect as she crossed the lawn towards the house, determined not to look back to see if Ned were still there. At the corner of the house, her resolve failed and she glanced over her shoulder as she turned the corner.

Ned was still there in the shadow of

the hedge, but, as she glanced his way, he turned abruptly and was gone.

Amelia's thoughts were in turmoil as she entered the house. She was totally unprepared for Louisa's verbal attack upon her as soon as she entered the hallway.

'Hah! So, there you are, miss! Returned at last from your assignation with your paramour! Ah, yes! Jesmond has told me all about discovering you in the rose garden! And the beating he received when he tried to remonstrate with you, poor lamb! And, from the look of your countenance, your lover has rejected you already! What did you expect? To be set up in style somewhere and given a carte-blanche?'

Louisa laughed harshly. 'That is all that will be left for you when word of your unseemly behaviour gets out! You are no better than a common trollop! And to think of all I have tried to do for you! Where are you going? I haven't finished with you yet!'

Amelia had silently turned away but

she paused as she reached the door.

'I am going to lie down in my room. I think perhaps I got up too soon after the mishap the other day. Please excuse me!'

Upstairs, she lay on her bed, her eyes staring sightlessly in her darkened room, unaware of the tears that coursed down her cheeks. What had happened? She had felt sure that Ned felt something for her, but she had obviously been mistaken. What a fool she felt! Louisa was right. She had behaved like a . . . She hiccupped. Surely not a 'trollop'! Surely Ned didn't think that of her. Was that why he had rejected her?

The door opened and Clara slipped into the room and seated herself on the edge of Amelia's bed.

'What happened?' she whispered with suppressed excitement. 'There was such a brouhaha when Jesmond stalked in with his bloodied nose! Did Mr Davenport hit him? What had he done? Louisa screamed all sorts of names at him! I didn't understand half of them but I realised they were bad because of her tone!'

She clasped hold of Amelia's hand. 'I know you're upset, but what did Mr Davenport say about me and Philip being friends. Can we visit them at their house?'

Amelia felt her throat tighten as she tried to speak. Silently, she shook her had from side to side on the pillow. 'I'm sorry, dearest.'

Clara's face fell. 'Oh! Was he very angry? Well, what did I tell you? Philip said how angry he could be when he drew that picture! So, now you know he was right!'

'No, no!' Amelia forced herself to sit up slightly. 'No, that's not the way it was.'

Struggling to control her voice, she told Clara what had happened in the rose garden and most of what she had overheard the previous night between Jesmond and Blake. 'So, I don't know what is to become of us,' she hiccupped. 'Blake was even prepared to give extra money to Jesmond to get me off their hands.

'You won't let them make me marry Jesmond instead of you, will you?' Clara asked in alarm.

'Of course not! I'd rather you ran away with Philip that have that happen!' Amelia exclaimed with much of her usual spirit returning. 'Oh!' She clasped a hand over her mouth as she realised what she had said. 'But, you won't, will you? I couldn't bear to have to contend with that on top of everything else!'

'No, of course not! Besides,' she giggled, glancing coyly through her lowered eyelashes, 'he hasn't asked me to . . . not yet!'

The following day started quietly. Not wanting to face Louisa too early in the day, Amelia sent Clara to ask Kate to bring their breakfast to her room and they talked over their plight in subdued mood.

'But we mustn't let it get us down!'

Amelia insisted. 'Once she breaks our spirit, we shall sink even lower . . . and I won't allow that to happen!'

They dressed mid-morning and descended downstairs to find the house quiet and peaceful.

'I'll send Kate with a tray for Mr Marsden, shall I, Miss Amelia?' Mrs Tranter asked when Amelia went to consult her about their luncheon. 'And maybe poor Mrs Forrester, too?'

Amelia knew that the servants would have heard much of the commotion of the previous day but would never make direct reference to it.

'I think that would be a good idea, Mrs Tranter,' she agreed pleasantly. She wasn't looking forward to her first meeting with either of the two and wasn't averse to putting it off as long as possible.

She and Clara were on their way to the dining room when Kate appeared from the kitchen, her face showing a mixture of concern and excitement.

'What is it, Kate?' Amelia asked.

'It's Mr Marsden, miss,' Kate replied. 'He's gone!'

'Gone?' Amelia echoed, not quite taking in what Kate had said. 'What do you mean, 'He's gone'? Gone where?'

'Well, I dunno, miss. But he's not there and neither are any of his clothes nor nothing. His room's empty!'

Amelia wondered if Jesmond's departure had been arranged the previous evening after Blake had learned of what had happened, but surely the servants would have been involved in his departure, however hurried? But that hadn't happened. They were as mystified as she was.

Louisa was equally mystified when informed of her brother's silent departure.

'Gone? Gone where?' she cried, echoing Amelia's reaction. 'How can he be gone? Something has happened to him? Have you had the grounds searched?'

'Well, no. All his things have gone, too. His room is bare,' Amelia explained.

'Wherever he has gone, he has taken everything with him.'

'And maybe other things, too,' she thought inwardly, a suspicion which became fact when Blake returned home and opened the safe that was concealed behind a large painting in the library . . . and declared that a bundle of bank notes had disappeared.

'I'll not have it! My brother isn't a thief!' Louisa wailed.

'I wouldn't count on that!' Blake said dryly. 'He had confessed to me how rolled-up he was and tried to squeeze some money out of me.'

'And you refused! How could you, Blake? You know what a run of bad luck he has had! Why didn't he come to me? I would have helped him!'

'I did give him some, but not the full amount he asked for or we'd have been brought to a standstill ourselves. I can't be throwing him a line forever, Louisa! He has to learn to curb his spending!'

'But where has he gone?'

'Probably on to richer pickings!'

'But, when will he be back? Oh, it's all your fault, you shameless hussy!' She turned on Amelia. 'You treated him abominably, trying to blacken his name with your lies! And now he has gone! Oh, I need to lie down!'

Throughout that day and the next, Louisa vented her spleen on the servants, demanding that work be done over and over again; chastising Kate for being far too frivolous in her manner to ever be thought of a lady's maid and found fault with every meal, saying the food was either too hot or too cold and completely unpalatable.

Everyone's nerves were stretched to the limit and both Mrs Tranter and Kate vowed they would throw down their aprons and leave if 'madam' didn't get off their backs!

'Except we wouldn't leave you and Miss Clara!' Mrs Tranter amended her statement.

They had nearly finished dinner that evening when they heard the bell at the front ringing.

'Who on earth could this be?' Louisa wondered aloud. 'It is an extremely unsocial hour to call! 'Oh!' She pushed back her chair and half rose from the table. 'It might be dear Jesmond returning to us!'

'Stay where you are, Louisa!' Blake commended with uncustomary force. 'Gerard will answer the door and announce our visitor.'

Louisa sank down again but her attention, and that of everyone else, was concentrated towards the murmuring of voices from the hall. Male voices.

Amelia felt a blush flaming her cheeks. It was Ned, she was sure of it.

For what reason would Ned call at such an inconvenient hour at this house where he knew himself to be unwelcome?

Gerard entered the dining room and went to the head of the table where Blake was sitting and leaned over his shoulder, murmuring quietly in his ear.

'You may announce your message to us all!' Louisa commanded sharply.

But Blake was wiping his lips with his napkin and rising from his chair. His expression was hard to read but he seemed perturbed and most of the colour had drained from his face.

'Excuse me for a few moments, my dear,' he murmured, stepping in front of Gerard and heading for the door.

'What is it?' Louisa demanded sharply, her anxiety growing.

But Blake waved his hand dismissively in her direction and stepped into the hall.

'Come to the library,' they heard him say.

The three ladies waited uneasily, giving up all pretence of eating. It was ten minutes before Blake reappeared. It was apparent that he was in shock. He went straight to Louisa's side.

'There's no easy way to say this,' he began, 'but it's bad news, I'm afraid. A man's body has been found in the coppice and Mr Davenport, our caller, fears it is that of Jesmond.'

# 10

'No . . . ooo!' Louisa rose to her feet as the scream erupted from her lips . . . and immediately fainted back into her chair.

Amelia hurried round to her side, where Blake was ineffectively patting her hand, clearly at a loss what to do. 'Pick her up and carry her into the sitting room,' Amelia instructed. 'Lay her on the sofa and stay at her side. I'll get her sal volatile.'

She found the small bottle and hurried into the sitting room where all the others were gathered round the still-prone figure. All were shocked by the announcement. How had it happened?

When Louisa revived and was seated propped against some cushions, she demanded to know what had happened.

'Are you sure you are up to it, my dear?' Blake asked in concern.

'I may as well hear it now as later,' Louisa said resignedly, her face white but now composed. She faced Ned. 'I suppose you found my brother's body, did you?' she said coldly. 'You have brought nothing but trouble to this family!'

'My men found him,' Ned said quietly, ignoring her antagonism towards him. 'His skull is crushed. I'm afraid it looks like he was beaten heavily on the head and his body hidden among some undergrowth.'

'Robbers, d'you think?' Amelia ventured.

'Possibly. He had no money on him.'

'It's all your fault!' Louisa suddenly accused Amelia. 'He wouldn't have left but for your licentious behaviour! And, yours! she continued, pointing an accusing finger at Ned. 'It's my belief you were in cahoots together and laid in wait for him! Yes, that must be it! Not content with bloodying his nose, you determined to kill him! Well, such wickedness won't go unpunished! Blake, apprehend this man and call the authorities!'

'No!' Clara cried and clutched hold of Amelia.

'I assure you, ma'am, it was no such thing,' Ned said calmly.

'Don't be absurd, Louisa!' Amelia retorted. 'I know you are distressed, but how could we have done it? We didn't even know he was leaving!'

But Louisa wasn't listening. Her eyes were wild with speculation.

'Maybe he wasn't leaving! Maybe you just made it look that way! I see it all! You've taken his clothes and hidden them somewhere!'

'Now, now, my dear,' Blake soothed, trying to put his arm around her shoulders.

But Louisa was too worked up to heed him.

'Leave me alone! It must have been them! He had exposed their liaison! They wanted to punish him! There was no-one else! Unless . . . '

She paused and stared accusingly at her husband. 'Unless . . . it was you?' Her voice took on a note of incredulity and dawning knowledge. 'Jesmond told me he knew! He was trying to blackmail you, wasn't he? He asked for money and threatened to expose you!'

Her eyes were wide with horror and she shrank away from her husband.

Blake looked round helplessly at the others.

'I'm sorry,' he apologised. 'It has all been too much for her. I'll send Gerard to bring the local doctor to administer a sleeping draught. Come, my dear. I will take you to your room to lie down.'

'No, no!' Louisa was now too hysterical to heed anyone. She waved her hands in frenzied movements, first at Blake as he tried to lift her and then at Amelia when she attempted to assist.

Amelia stepped back, calmly taking hold of the bell-pull by the mantelpiece. 'I will send for Mathilde. She will attend to you, Louisa. You will feel safe with her.

Blake glanced helplessly at everyone as they awaited Mathilde's arrival and then followed his wife and maid upstairs.

'So, what was that about?' Ned asked Amelia when the door had closed upon the three of them.

Amelia shook her head thoughtfully. 'I'm not sure,' she murmured. 'She's right. Jesmond did say something.' She searched her memory. 'I don't think I told you this bit, Clara. I had dismissed it as Jesmond playing games. He said something about hearing that Blake had 'worked his way into a fortune' but he promised to keep quiet about it if Blake made it worth his while. Of course, Blake dismissed it as nonsense.

'Then Jesmond said he had contacts at Westminster who only needed him to 'nod the wink' at them and they would say what they knew. He mentioned a name . . . Bradshaw . . . Rupert Bradshaw . . . and asked if it meant anything to him. Blake said no but Jesmond laughed and threatened that Blake needed to watch his back. I wonder what he's been up to?'

Ned was thoughtful. He knew Rupert Bradshaw. He had been one of the secretaries to Spenser Perceval, the former Prime Minister, who had been assassinated in the lobby of the House of Commons two years earlier. Lord Liverpool, his successor, had brought in his own team of secretaries and Rupert Bradshaw had found himself lower down the pecking line. Had he revealed some knowledge from his former position that had enabled Blake Forrester to . . . what had Miss Haverton said, 'to work his way into a fortune'?

The only fortune that he knew Forrester had gained was the Haverton estate! But that had been entirely legal. Everyone knew he was next-in-line after Ralph Haverton. The tragedy was that the son had been killed in seemingly shameful circumstances, thus hastening the death of his elderly father. But the outcome would have been the same whatever the circumstances of Ralph's death. He wasn't married and thus had no legal heir. So, what had Forrester done?

One thing he was sure of. Ralph Haverton was no traitor!

But, what could he do about it? He had spent the past six months intent on keeping a low profile . . . disappearing without trace had been his hope. However, he was beginning to fear it had been to no avail. If his suspicions were correct, his cover had been penetrated and his plans about to be blown away.

He looked at the lovely young woman at his side, her eyes intent on his as she awaited the outcome of his musings. She and her sister had bravely borne the double blow of the deaths of their father and brother and the added blow of losing their home. How could he not try to do whatever lay in his power to try to at least show that her faith in her brother had not been in vain? He couldn't. Not even at the risk of his own endeavours going awry.

His mind made up, he smiled. Unthinkingly, he reached out and let a curling tendril of Amelia's hair entwine itself around his finger.

'I need to go to town for a few days,' he murmured. 'Keep what you have told me to yourselves.' He included Clara in his gaze. 'And keep within the safety of your own grounds. There is bound to be an investigation into Marsden's death. Answer what questions they ask but don't move into speculation. I have already spoken to the local magistrate on my own behalf. My men will take care of anything else until my return.'

He withdrew his finger from the curl and watched it spring back into place in front of her left ear. He was aware of the door opening and he made his bow as Blake re-entered the room.

'I must bid you goodnight, ladies, and you too, Forrester. The local magistrate knows where the body of your brother-in-law is. It will be restored to you as soon as he sees fit. Goodnight!'

The house seemed empty when he had gone. Blake was in no mood for conversation and, as soon as the doctor had made his visit and left medication for Louisa, the two girls retired upstairs in sombre mood.

Below, stairs, the servants made their own speculations and gossiped well into the late hours, wondering what changes, if any, this latest event would make on their lives.

The following day, Blake told Vernon that his uncle had suffered a fatal accident but didn't go into details.

No mention was made of Louisa's wild accusations and, since she slept soundly throughout that day, ministered to solely by her maid, it was the following day when the first repercussions fell upon the household.

'We shall all go into deep mourning!' Louisa declared. 'You still have your mourning clothes, do you not?'

'Ye . . . es,' Amelia replied, remembering how drab they had been for over twelve months but realising the necessity.

'That's not fair!' Clara declared with great feeling. 'We hardly knew him!'

'That is beside the point!' Louisa snapped. 'He was my only brother and deserves the deepest respect of us all, especially when . . . Oh . . . h!'

'That's fine, Louisa,' Amelia hastily assured her, glaring at Clara. 'He was our cousin, after all!'

'How could you agree so quickly?' Clara demanded when they were on their own. 'At least you might have pressed for half-mourning! Lilac can be quite becoming.'

'Just until after the funeral and maybe the first month or so,' Amelia tried to commiserate. 'It is expected, you know.'

'But he was such a clown! And I hate black! I vowed never to wear it again! It will be hypocritical of us!'

'Louisa is very upset. Remember how we felt when Ralph and Papa died. We must do as she says for now!'

Late in the afternoon two days later,

Amelia went upstairs to see how Clara was feeling. Her sister had excused herself from the luncheon table, pleading a slight headache and Amelia hadn't seen her since. She found Clara's black dress thrown into the corner of her room and, when she opened her wardrobe, she knew at once that her sister's favourite day gown was missing.

'Where has the naughty child hidden herself?' Amelia spoke aloud. It was obvious that she was not here in the house and a search of the garden proved just as fruitless.

'I supposed you're looking for Miss Clara,' Mrs Tranter observed, when Amelia re-entered the house through the kitchen door. 'I saw her slipping off through the kitchen garden just after luncheon, while everyone else was still at the table, wearing her pretty sprigged muslin frock. Eh, now! Don't be cross at her! She likes to be free . . . like a butterfly.'

'Don't we all!' Amelia glowered. 'It's not the frock I mind so much. Though it is naughty of her! But, Mr Davenport warned us to keep within our own boundaries until Jesmond's killer is found.'

'Well, I don't suppose he'd hang around here!' Mrs Tranter voiced as her opinion. 'Shall I ask Gerard or Sam to look out for her?'

'Yes. But I have an idea where she might be.'

Amelia turned about and made straight for the stile by the side of the spinney, confident of seeing her sister in animated sign-conversation with Philip, but she was disappointed. A pink hair-ribbon that she knew to be Clara's lay on the ground. It was dry to the touch, so she knew it hadn't been there since their previous visit.

While she was considering what to do, she heard rustling among the shrubs within the woodland and the low murmur of men's voices coming closer. She looked hastily about for some place to hide but hadn't taken more than one step when a large black dog bounded out of the thicket and leaped towards her. It skidded to a halt no more than a yard away, its teeth bared in an angry snarl.

Amelia froze. She liked dogs and, on the whole, they responded well to her, but not this one. Each tiny movement from her initiated a rumbling growl in the dog's throat. She could neither retreat nor proceed.

A voice from the thick called, 'Down, boy!' and the dog dropped with its belly on the ground, his muzzle resting on his front paws.

When Amelia risked turning her head to see who was coming, she recognised something familiar in the man who emerged room the spinney and, as another man appeared at his side, she noticed hefty cudgels in their hands. Seeing them together side-by-side, she suddenly realised where she had seen them before. They were the two men who had frightened her and Clara when they had been out picking blackberries . . . and had stolen their picnic!

Alarm immediately seized her. In rising panic, she started to back away but the dog emitted a warning growl.

'No!' she cried, poised for flight.

The dog growled again and, as she hesitated, she saw the men lower their cudgels and regard her with sheepish recognition.

'We've met before!' she said tersely, a sense of calm overcoming her anxiety.

'Aye, miss!' one man greeted her, doffing his cap and nudging the other man to do the same. 'Don't be afeared, miss. Here, boy!'

The dog rose to its feet, wagging its tail, and loped over to the man.

The men seemed slightly embarrassed by the situation. 'We're sorry about frightening you afore . . . and the other miss. We was hungry, see!'

'And now you're poaching rabbits or some such?' she enquired, trying to stop her voice from trembling.

'Eh, no, miss! We're honest men! We works for the capt'n, now. He took us on, we'd served in his platoon.' They exchanged worried glances. 'We found t'body t'other day and we're keeping watch for . . . strangers.'

'He certainly likes his privacy,' Amelia commented, still recovering from her terror of anticipating being mauled by the dog. 'I would like to speak with Mr Davenport. Has he returned from town yet?'

'No, miss. Though he's due any day. But you shouldn't be here, miss. It ain't safe! There's been intruders round about . . . such as them as hurt t'other dog a few weeks ago . . . an' mebee killed t'young fellow!'

Reminded of that, Amelia forgot her fear of her own position. 'Yes, I know. Mr Davenport warned us. That is why I am concerned about my sister. I don't know where she is,' she cried, her voice trembling as she uttered the last words.

The men glanced at each other in dismay, obviously not knowing how to deal with a distressed lady of her class.

'Tha'd best come with us, miss. Master Philip might know something!'

'Yes, indeed he might!' Amelia responded with renewed vigour, her former terror ebbing away as she recalled her earlier suspicions.

She climbed the stile and tramped across the meadow with growing expectation of seeing her sister within ten minutes or so and was rehearsing her admonishment. As they entered the stable yard, the dog bounded ahead, his tail wagging and his bark sounding his welcome. Amelia's heart leaped. Was Ned back?

But it wasn't Ned's voice she heard welcome the dog. In fact, it was a voice she hadn't heard before. It was young and heavily accented.

'Here, boy!'

'Viens ici! Ah, tu es mechant, non!'

She halted in amazement.

'Philip! You're talking!'

# 11

'Oh!' Philip's face was a picture. A mixture of guilt, rebellion . . . and a certain amount of wildness! The wildness that Amelia knew had drawn Clara to him. He shrugged his shoulders and smiled. 'Je regret . . . I mean, I am sorry, Madam! I not want to . . . deceive . . . but Ned . . . he say I 'ave to!'

'But, why?'

Philip shrugged again.

'I am French.'

'But, what has that . . . ?'

A horseman galloped into the yard, cutting Amelia's puzzlement short.

'Ned!'

Ned reined in his horse and swung himself down from the saddle, tossing the reins to Thomas.

His face was stern and Amelia knew he was angry that she had disobeyed his request to them not to visit.

'Miss Haverton! I wondered if I would find you here! There's quite a hue and cry going on back at the manor.'

'Clara went missing,' she faltered.

Ned turned his attention to Philip, his eyebrow raised questioningly.

The youth shrugged his shoulders and looked resentful. He spoke rapidly in a language that Amelia couldn't understand and she looked at Ned enquiringly.

'Speak in English, Philippe!' Ned snapped.

Philip threw him a surly glance. 'Clara is my friend, yet you forbid me to see her. Why should I obey you? You are not my father!'

'No, your father is dead and you are in the same danger!' He turned to Amelia. 'I'm sorry, Miss Haverton. I had hoped not to involve you and your sister in any of the dangers our situation presents. Philippe, it seems, has other ideas! Stay where you are!' he barked, as Philip turned to storm away.

Amelia made a gesture of compassion towards Philip, which Ned interrupted.

'You think I am too harsh with the lad, Miss Haverton? If you had seen the senseless slaughter that has swept across France in the past few years you would not think so! His parents were dragged from their home to a mockery of a trial and summarily executed. But for the bravery of faithful servants, Philippe would have suffered the same fate. As it was, they kept him hidden until we were able to bring him to safety in England. The servants are now dead also and the chateau vandalised. These men are ruthless and relentless. They will never give up!'

'And they know that Philip is here?'

'I don't know. All we know is that someone has been watching the place.'

'And Clara has disappeared!'

'Captain Davenport, sir!'

'What is it, Dickon?'

The man was clutching a pink

bonnet that Amelia instantly recognised.

'That's Clara's! Where did you find it?'

Dickon also held out a small scroll of paper.

'T'was tied to the ribbons, sir! Can't make head nor tail of what it says.'

Ned unfolded the paper and swiftly read it, his lips tightening. 'It says they've got Clara, I'm afraid. They are willing to do an exchange at the bridge at seven o'clock.'

His left hand was already under her right elbow, supporting her and now she swayed towards him, feeling weak with shock. She rested her head against his chest and felt him clasp her to him.

Philip spoke again in his own language and this time, Ned didn't rebuke him. Instead, he replied in the same way, his voice rough with impatience. Then, his voice gentled and he touched the boy's arm as he spoke some more.

Amelia looked up at Ned.

'What did he say?'

'He said he would go in exchange.'

'But, they'll kill him!'

'Yes. They want to eliminate all legal heirs to the confiscated properties, but I told him we would try to rescue Clara first.'

Amelia's hand rose to her mouth, her fingers spread across her lips. 'She might be killed! Oh, Ned! I'm so frightened!'

'I know. Now, I want you to take Philippe inside and make a large pan of broth. We'll all need it by the time we get back.'

Amelia looked alarmed. 'I've never made broth!'

Ned laughed. 'Then, here's a good time to learn! Don't worry. I have already taught Philippe. It is a typical campaign menu. He will show you.'

Waiting was hard. Amelia's imagination worked overtime and she knew it was no easier for Philip, or Philippe, as she now knew his name to be. Each time the large clock in the hall chimed the quarter hour, she exchanged an anxious glance with him.

At last, they heard one of the dogs barking and Philippe ran to the kitchen door and peered out into the darkness. Clara was the first to run forward. She threw herself into Philippe's arms and then ran to Amelia.

'Oh, it was horrible, Amelia! I was so frightened . . . and then all that shooting! I was sure I'd be killed! And one of Mr Davenport's men was hurt and one of my captors was shot. I thought I'd never see you again!'

Amelia held her while she sobbed out her terror and then led her to a kitchen chair to sit down. Ned calmly dressed the bullet wound in Thomas's shoulder and then dusted the cleaned wound with basilicum powder while Philippe was firing questions at him about how the matter had proceeded.

She saw Ned murmuring something to Dickon, who nodded, snatched up a cob of bread and slipped back outside.

The bowls of broth were well

received and Amelia found it extraordinary to be seated on rough wooden chairs around the kitchen table with a group of ex-soldiers who were clearly minding their manners because of her and Clara's presence.

The meal over, Thomas went somewhere to rest and the other men cleared the table.

'I suppose we had better be thinking of returning home,' Amelia said at length but without enthusiasm. As she spoke the outer door opened and, to their immense surprise, Mrs Tranter and Kate were ushered into the kitchen.

'Oh! Mrs Tranter! Have you come to take us home?'

'Eh, no, miss! It's pandemonium back there!'

'Oh, dear! Because of our absence? I'm sorry, Ned. I didn't think to ask if you could send word of our safety to Louisa.'

'Eh, it's got nowt to do with you and Miss Clara,' Mrs Tranter exclaimed. 'It's Mr Forrester. The militia came and took him away. Mrs Forrester was hysterical! It seems he's been charged with treason and murder!'

Ned eventually suggested that Mrs Tranter and Kate go upstairs to prepare two rooms for Amelia and Clara and he filled in the answers to the barrage of questions that the two sisters hurled at him.

'I'm sorry,' he said. 'I didn't expect everything to move so quickly. You see, Miss Haverton, when you mentioned Rupert Bradshaw, I recognised the name. My father, er, has a seat in the House of Lords and has suspected Bradshaw of being involved with one or two unsavoury episodes. As one of the previous prime minister's secretaries Bradshaw was privy to much confidential information and, when Spenser Perceval was assassinated, he lost his plum job. Unwisely, he decided to supplement his income by making spurious use of the information he knew.'

'But what has that to do with Blake?'

Amelia asked. 'He wasn't in Spenser Perceval's Party. I know Louisa likes to inflate his importance but he's really in quite a junior position.'

'That may be so, but the confidential information that is relevant here are the names of some of our undercover agents who were on active service around the time of Perceval's death.' He paused, before adding, 'One of whom was your brother, Ralph.'

'Ralph? An undercover agent? You mean he was a spy?'

'All countries have them. It's one of the ways we find out what our enemies are up to. If you are spying for your own country, it is considered an honourable role. It only becomes dishonourable when you betray your country . . . as Ralph was made to seem to have done!'

Amelia drew in her breath sharply. 'So, what did Blake do?'

'Bradshaw told him where Ralph was acting undercover and the nature of the operation, and your cousin leaked the information to the enemy. He knew that with Ralph out of the way while he was still unmarried, he was next in line to inherit your home. It might not have been for many years . . . but circumstances went his way. Your father was elderly and the shock and disgrace of Ralph's supposed treason hastened his death.'

'Blake caused Ralph's death?' Amelia whispered.

'I'm afraid so. The enemy knew exactly where Ralph was operating, dates, the timing . . . everything.'

'Did Louisa know, too?' Clara asked incredulously.

'I don't know where or not she knew all the details at the time it happened but she certainly knew what her husband had done afterwards.'

'How would Jesmond have discovered it?'

'Maybe from his sister, or directly from Bradshaw. Men like him try to milk both ends of the information.'

'Only Blake wouldn't pay!'

'He was probably paying Bradshaw for his silence, too, so, if Marsden, when he knew he wouldn't get his hands on your money, tried to push him too far, all Forrester could think of doing was silencing him . . . for ever.'

'Poor Louisa!' Amelia murmured.

'Serve her right, more likely!' Clara declared.

'Yes, but she's lost her husband, her brother . . . and now, possibly, her home.'

'No more than we lost!'

'I know, and I'm reminded how dreadful it was.' She turned to Ned. 'Will she lose Moreton Manor?'

Ned shook his head. 'I don't know. Possibly not. Forrester was the legal heir. Now, it will probably pass to their son, unless the crown claims it if the treason is proved. It is possible that the crown could seize control and bestow it as a favour. It is likely to be the centre of a legal wrangle for years to come.'

'Could it be returned to us?'

'I don't know. I have asked my father

to speak on your behalf.'

Amelia felt a faint sense of hope that Moreton Manor might be hers again one day. But what was to happen to her and Clara in the meantime?

Later that night, after Amelia had dismissed Kate from her room, she heard a faint scratching at her door. She expected it to be Clara wanting to snuggle in with her for comfort, but, when she didn't come in and the sound was repeated, she wrapped a shawl around her shoulders and opened the door.

It was Ned.

'May I speak with you privately?' he asked. 'I know it is unconventional, but I must move Philippe to a new place of safety tomorrow. We need to leave without trace in order to keep ahead of anyone.'

'Oh, of course.' Her voice revealed her sadness and disappointment. 'Where will you go?'

'I have a place in mind. My father will help.'

'But, will you have to keep running and hiding for ever?'

'For a while, yes, but not for ever. The tide is turning. The new regime is as flawed as the old and some of their leaders have already been discredited. Soon, the dispossessed ones will be able to return and claim what is legally theirs, if they are still alive.'

'And then your task will be over.'

'Yes, but it may be a few years ahead. The thing is, I wondered . . . ' Heavens, he felt more nervous than during a campaign on the eve of a battle! ' . . . I wondered if you would care to come with us? And Clara, of course. And your cook and your maid.'

'C . . . come with you?' Amelia stammered, her cheeks flaring.

'You see, once we've gone tomorrow, we'll have to cover our tracks so well that I wouldn't be able to contact you until I deem it safe for Philippe to return to France, and, each time we meet . . . ' He looked embarrassed. ' . . . my heart seems to leap around my body or stop beating all together . . . and I sense that perhaps you feel the same way.'

He paused, looking hopefully at her.

Amelia's heart somersaulted within her. 'Oh, I do!' she breathed.

'And it will give Clara and Philippe time to get to know each other and see if their friendship develops . . . for they believe themselves in love already,' he continued, as if he had still to persuade her.

'Yes, we'll come!' she declared more firmly, raising her head to look straight into his eyes.

'You will? Oh, my darling girl!'

He drew her into his arms and tilted her chin. 'I'll never love you more than I do right now!'

He kissed her lips tenderly and felt her response quicken beneath his touch. Oh, how he would delight in nurturing her desire into passionate expression! 'And I took the liberty of obtaining a special licence whilst I was in town,' he murmured as his lips traced their way across her cheek and nuzzled around her ear, such a tiny, pretty ear, he inconsequentially noticed.

Amelia arched her neck sensuously, revelling in the sensations that were coursing around her body.

'Licence?' she murmured, thinking that she had never dreamed that anything could feel like this!

'Marriage licence. We won't be able to spend three weeks in residence anywhere while our banns are read.'

'Banns? Marriage licence? You are asking me to marry you? Oh! I thought . . . '

Her cheeks flamed again.

Ned cupped her cheeks in his hands and smiled wondrously.

'You would have come without marriage?'

Amelia felt a wave of shame wash over her. Now, he must surely despise her! Oh, how could she have been so foolish? As if Ned would seek to dishonour her!

She tried to drop her gaze, but Ned

held her firmly, now cupping her chin with one hand and stroking down her hair with the other.

Surely it was admiration that shone from his eyes, not scorn — and she felt emboldened to say, 'I would have done, rather than lose the chance of loving you, but I would prefer to be married . . . that is, if you don't mind?'

Ned roared with laughter. 'I don't mind at all, and, d'you know, I was mistaken when I said I would never love you more than at that moment — for I love you more already!'

FAITH FOR THE FUTURE
A CHANGE OF HEART
ILLUSIONS OF LOVE
A DIVIDED INHERITANCE

# A TIME TO DANCE

## Eileen Stafford

Deborah thinks that nothing exciting happens in wartime Bristol. But then the Americans arrive, preparing to fight in occupied Europe. And for Deborah, everything changes. She finds excitement when she meets Warren and falls in love. But her romantic dreams are shattered when her father sends her away to live with her aunt in Exmouth. And more heartbreak follows when she feels forced to seek refuge in London. At the end of the war — can she ever find happiness again?

# HIS LITTLE GIRL

## Liz Fielding

Staying alone at her brother-in-law's cottage on a stormy night, Dora finds an intruder in the house, a man called John Gannon. He's clearly a man on the run, but Dora is charmed by him — and the adorable little girl in his arms. She decides to help Gannon, a devoted father, willing to do anything to keep Sophie safe. Too bad the only thing keeping Dora safe from Gannon is his misconception that she is Richard's wife . . .

# LEGACY OF LOVE

## Dorothy Taylor

Bookseller Kay Deacon learns that she has been left part of the late Tobias Garner's collection of antique books on condition she brings his records up to date. So when Tobias's nephew Marshall Garner accuses her of cultivating the old man's affections, Kay resolves to carry out Tobias's wishes and prove that she is not a gold digger. But when she begins to find herself entangled in a web of deceit, her own life is in danger . . .

# THE VALIANT FOOL

## Valerie Holmes

Emma Frinton, a captain's daughter, is forced to live in reduced circumstances in a humble cottage in the small fishing village of Ebton, when the French imprison her father. Emma and her mother, Lydia, accept leaving their beloved home in Whitby, but neither of them anticipates the consequences of Emma's kindly actions when she stumbles across an injured man on the dunes. In saving Montgomery Wild's life, she unwittingly finds the key to unlock their family's future.